WHERE SUGARPLUMS SHIMMER

Other Books by C. L. Fails

A Spoonful of Sugarplums

So Okay...Treasured Stories from the Life of James M. Robinson, Sr.

My Magical Story Journal

The Secret World of Raine the Brain Series

The Ella Books Series

The Christmas Cookie Books

WHERE SUGARPLUMS SHIMMER

A NOVEL

C. L. FAILS

LaunchCrate Publishing
Kansas City, KS

Where Sugarplums Shimmer
Written by C. L. Fails

LaunchCrate Publishing
Kansas City, KS
info@launchcrate.com
www.launchcrate.com

Ordering Information:
Quantity sales. Special discounts are available on quantity purchases by corporations, associations, and others. For details, contact the publisher at the email address above. Orders by U.S. trade bookstores and wholesalers.

Library of Congress Control Number: 2020915843

Hardcover ISBN: 978-1-947506-17-6
Paperback ISBN: 978-1-947506-18-3

Printed in the United States of America
10 9 8 7 6 5 4 3 2 1

First Edition

For those of you in search of seeds of hope, may you find
them and plant them for others to discover as well.

"...our relationship had become fully engulfed in flames. I definitely wouldn't have predicted this given the way the tide turned in our favor...But regardless of what I had anticipated, it didn't change the outcome."

Calendar of Events

Calendar of Events

Where Sugarplums Shimmer

Chapter 1

Christmas Eve

By the time Easter arrived, our relationship had become fully engulfed in flames. I definitely wouldn't have predicted this given the way the tide turned in our favor on Christmas Eve. But regardless of what I had anticipated, it didn't change the outcome.

Things moved swiftly between Dr. Chris and I. We had bumped into each other at The Fresh Grind on a Friday, and just 11 days later I was fighting the urge to propose marriage. I knew it the moment I caught her from hitting the floor. This was just different. She was different. My heart was different.

Just three dates was all it took and I knew. She knew. Even my mom knew and I hadn't seen her since July. But life has this way of testing your desires, to see if you're willing to fight for what you say you want. I didn't see it coming at all, that test.

I call myself closing a chapter of life so we'd have no more distractions. She had stumbled upon me in the throws of an intimate conversation with my ex. When a dear friend helped me discover what might have happened, I went to clear things up with Dr. Chris, and found her body intertwined with another man - in much the same manner as the relationship door I had just closed. I can't lie about it. That knocked the wind right out of me. I questioned everything I thought to be true.

Dr. Chris and I almost fell back on old habits and allowed the world to sweep us up in its web of confusion, but the moment I saw the video of the two of us at the tree farm, I knew we were designed for each other. She gazed at me the way my mom snuck glimpses of my father when she thought he wasn't looking. I hadn't seen it while we were out there because I was too busy sawing down Randolph. But there was no hiding it in that video. She was my heart outside of my body. She was love. So, when I put my pride aside and replied to her text, I was hopeful that she would still be receptive to me. When she replied, I heaved a sigh of relief and the sense of longing I had just questioned, returned like high tide.

I yearned for another glimpse into her soul, to see her the way I had on the day we met, but all I had were my memories and the photo of the two of us at Union Station. The more I gazed that photo, the more I remembered just how different this relationship was. I was prepared to lock it down and provide a hedge of protection for my heart outside my body. So, I set that photo as my phone's lock screen background as a reminder and called it a night.

I awoke on Christmas Eve, knowing at the very least that I had to see her before I headed out of town to visit my parents for Christmas. I sent my mom a text to let her know that I'd be home for Christmas and shifted my attention to Dr. Chris. In a text prepared to send her way, I had just finished typing the words, "good morning," when I received her message. "Dear Santa, just spoke with Marley. She told me her Christmas wish." I deleted my message and replied as swiftly as my fingers would let me.

"Open your gift."

I received her reply, "okay," and now with the reassurance that the gift would communicate how special she was to me, I hurriedly finished packing my bag for the 3 and a half hour road trip from Kansas City to Fayetteville. I checked my phone, waiting for her follow up. Nothing. All of the not knowing felt like a someone was stirring up my nerves into a batch of homemade pancakes. The longer I sat, the more my anxiety began to swell. Then I received it, a notification from my Sugarplum for sugarplums. They had brought us together and I hoped they would be the bridge that reconnected us after our misunderstanding. That was my cue to leave. Almost immediately thereafter, I received her text, asking if I was still in the city. *Is she just going to pretend like she didn't see the gift? Did she not like it? Was it too much? Has she even seen it yet?* My mind was racing. At the very least, I needed to know if she had opened the gift. I was wearing my heart on my sleeve and it felt like she was toying with it. "Did you open the gift?" I asked her.

When she said no, I didn't have any words. All I could send in return were question marks as I rustled through my home checking to ensure that the doors were locked and the windows were all closed. "I need to see you before I open this, Charlie." I grabbed my bag, set the house alarm and headed out the front door to hop in my pickup truck, Chief. Waiting for me were the flowers I had picked up for her the day before. I smiled knowing we were on our way back to Hope Gardens. I just needed to tell Chris I was coming.

"I'm about to leave Chris," I told her as I put Chief in reverse and backed out of the driveway. My phone buzzed twice before Chief was fully in the street. I assumed it was my mom's reply and made a mental note to check that after I sorted things out with Dr. Chris.

The trip to Hope Gardens took a bit longer than normal with the detour to The Fresh Grind. When I arrived, Marlo greeted me with a dap and asked Susan to page Dr. Chris. He told me about his new job and explained the confusion-sparking embrace that I had seen. I owed Chris an explanation and I could hardly wait to do that, but she wasn't responsive to Susan's call. I asked Marlo if she was with a patient, but he assured me that he had just left her in her office. Something was wrong and I hoped that I could fix it. Susan beckoned me to the intercom system so I could call Dr. Chris for myself.

"Paging Dr. Chris to the Family Room. Dr. Chris to the Family Room." I returned to my conversation with Marlo, internally hoping that would do the trick.

In the distance I heard the sound of a door flinging open and smacking the wall, before the quick tapping of two feet pacing along the linoleum echoed throughout the halls of the hospital wing. It was only a few seconds, but I was sweating it out, waiting to see if the traipsing feet belonged to Dr. Chris.

Her voice, full of angst, "Charlie?" sounded as though she were surprised to see me. *I had told her I was on the way.* I turned to see her, my hands still holding the hot cider and my heart coveting what my eyes beheld. I was so relieved to see her face in person, and I was prepared to hug her with the ciders that I held up for her to see, but Marlo stepped in giving me the chance to fully hold her, protect her, and pour my love into her.

I'm not sure if I picked her up or if she leapt into my arms, but I do remember a momentum induced spin that I needed to slow. I just wanted to see her face. I wanted to see into her soul again. I wanted her to see into mine. I was certain that it would explain far more than words could ever do. As I guided her softly back to the ground and gazed upon her face, freshly washed with tears, my heart nearly broke into a million fragmented shards of glass. I wiped them away as gently as I could and placed my forehead lovingly on hers. *This woman.*

She tried to explain what happened but I stopped her. It honestly didn't matter. What was important in that moment was that I saw her and she saw me. We were in the middle of a hospital, but it felt like we were alone. Everyone else had melted away. She asked about Oakley and I told her in the simplest way possible that I had asked her to stop calling me. Then I blurted it out. "Come with me."

I don't even know where it came from, or what spirit prompted me to say it, but there I was baring my entire heart, risking embarrassment and asking Dr. Chris to join me on a road trip to visit my parents. I hadn't intended on asking her that question when I left the house. I hadn't planned to put her in such a precarious situation, but here we were. She nodded immediately, but I wasn't sure what that meant to her, so twice I asked for clarification, before she emphatically whispered yes into my ear. Elated, I hummed to her, in the middle of the hallway before she, Dr. Chris - a woman who just days before had told me that nobody wanted to hear her singing, began singing what have now become my favorite lyrics. All I could do was kiss her right there, in front of her co-workers and patients, like tomorrow wasn't promised and I needed her to know I loved her today.

After I realized that everyone was applauding us, I was slightly embarrassed, but it wasn't enough to stop me from showing this woman just how much I cared.

She smiled at me and grabbed my hand, turning to formally introduce me to Marlo, who presented us with the sugarplum laced ciders.

"I feel like I know you already," he told me. "Chris has shared so much about you." I turned to the good doctor and smiled, lacing my fingers between hers.

"Thank you - for everything, Marlo," I replied, nodding in his direction before kissing Dr. Chris on her temple as she leaned her weight into me.

From the tiniest voice within eye-shot came a joyous exclamation, "Dr. Chris!" It was Marley, the patient I had visited with during the night of the jubilee. Our fingers still intertwined, Dr. Chris led me to the threshold of Marley's room.

"Marley, can I introduce you to someone?" she asked, knowing full well that we had already met but trying to keep my Santa cover under wraps.

"Yes, yes!" she shouted, inspiring laughter from Susan and anyone else within earshot.

"This is Mr. Hughes and I think he's your Christmas wish."

"Can I hug you?" she asked, her question pointed more towards me than Dr. Chris. I slowly let go of Chris' hand and stepped closer to her bedside. Trying to avert my eyes from hers, I gently wrapped one arm around Marley and hugged her shoulders. She reached up and cupped my face with her hands, turning my head from one side to the other, seemingly studying every millimeter of me. Still holding my cider, I dropped to one knee so she wouldn't have to reach up quite so high. Then, knowing I'd be unable to avoid it for much longer, I raised my eyes to meet hers. She gasped and whispered, "Santa?"

"Shhhhh," I urged quietly. "She doesn't know."

Suddenly sounding sad, and slightly afraid of the answer, she faintly asked, "Will she have to leave with you or can she stay here?"

Under my breath I replied, "She can do whatever she wants. I'll love her wherever she is."

"Always?" she continued to whisper.

I nodded, "As long as there is breath in my lungs, Marley."

"Thank you, Santa," she whispered before leaning in to hug me.

"What are you two whispering about over there?" Dr. Chris asked from the doorway.

"Nothing," the two of us exclaimed in unison. I nodded at Marley, stood to my feet and returned to the doorway with Dr. Chris.

"It was nice to meet you, Marley!" I said aloud.

Giving me a thumbs up, Marley replied, "It was nice to meet you too for the very first time ever, Mr. Hughes."

Dr. Chris chuckled and quickly stepped in the room to cross pinkies with Marley before they wished each other a good day.

"Are you ready?" Dr. Chris asked me. I nodded at her before waving goodbye to Marley. By that time the crowd had dispersed, so the two of us were able to walk back to Dr. Chris' office uninterrupted. She opened her palm towards the chair in front of her desk while she returned to move her task chair. That's when I noticed the feel in the room. There it was greeting me, the box, the paper thrown astray, the scene looked chaotic and harried. I wondered what had happened that brought her to tears, so I asked.

"What happened?"

"What happened when, Charlie?" she asked, her eyes in search of mercy.

"Before you were paged, what happened before you were paged?" I asked reaching out for her hand. Scooching her chair forward, she held my hand in hope. My eyes acknowledged her hesitance before she bowed her head in response.

"I thought you had slipped away, unwilling to see me before you left. I was sitting in my chair and realized that I was stewing in the pot of my own making and I only hoped that I hadn't irrevocably damaged us." I nodded and listened as she continued, "Marley had given me the gift of perspective, and I wasn't even sure that I deserved this," she said holding up the empty box. "I had to give myself a pep talk to open it, Charlie." I nodded again. "I thought things were done and the worst part about it? I'd have this tragically beautiful reminder of what I almost had, what I let fall through my fingers because I couldn't get out of my own way. I held my breath as I raised the lid, and your words hit me in my gut - 'I'll fight for you for as long as there is breath in my lungs.' I couldn't help the stream of tears that started to fall from my eyes. When I saw the ornament, I was in full ugly cry mode. Then I read the inscription," she pulled the ornament from her coat pocket and lovingly ran her fingers over the words etched into the back, "'To hang on every Randolph we find,' and I wept for the love that I had lost."

I squeezed her hand, "Chris."

"Then I heard your voice and I promised I'd do everything in my power to stay present with you."

It was dusty in her office, and that dust, mysteriously crept up into my eye ducts. I wanted so much to tell her, to ask her, but I knew it wasn't the right time. She had my heart and that wasn't going to change. "I told you I was coming."

"You told me you were about to leave, right after I asked if you were still in the city."

I picked up my phone to reread our text exchange when I noticed the two unread messages I had received when I was leaving. One was from Dr. Chris. The other, was from my mom, asking if I was going to be bringing Dr. Chris with me.

"You're right," I told her after scrolling back through our conversation. "I'm sorry I wasn't clear."

"Charlie, there's no need to apologize."

"There is, Chris." I proceeded to apologize for jumping to conclusions and stonewalling her instead of asking questions. I apologized for not giving her the benefit of the doubt. My voice quivered, "I know your heart the same way you know mine." I cleared my throat before continuing, "Also, I wasn't trying to put you on the spot when I asked you to come with me today. It's okay if you don't -" she cut me off before I could finish.

"Charlie, I wanted to come with you - I want to. I'm glad you asked."

"Good, 'cause it looks like my mom asked if you were coming with me. I just saw her text. But now that she knows I've read it, I need to reply," I chuckled, hoping it would help to lighten the mood.

A look of confusion fell upon her face, "Your mom knows about me?"

"Patient-client confidentiality?"

She smiled, "Doctor-patient confidentiality only works between a doctor and a patient, sir."

"Stethoscope. Use the stethoscope!" I urged, hoping it would save me from having to divulge an answer.

Laughing, she refused and reiterated her question. "Your mom knows about me?"I nodded. "So what did you tell her, Charlie?"

"Well…" I stalled. Her big brown eyes coerced me into confessing that I had called my mom back the night of the Jubilee.

Dr. Chris leaned in across the table, "She knew that you loved me from the sound of your voice?"

"Yeah, that and probably the way I described you," I said, scratching the back of my head and looking everywhere in her office except directly at her. That felt too vulnerable.

Dr. Chris hid her face in embarrassment, "Charlie."

She and I had much to catch up on but I was in no hurry. In fact, we would still need to wait a few more hours (the duration of her shift) before we could return to her condo so she could pack a bag. So there we sat, chatting about everything and nothing all at once. It was so natural, so comfortable. *This woman.*

Once her shift was over, I followed her back to the condo, parking in her guest spot below ground and riding the elevator up with her, past the 10 floors of business space and up to the 2nd floor of residential space. Each floor we passed took my mind back to Unit 227. It felt like a full week had elapsed since I'd walked her back upstairs after the Jubilee. I refused to step inside two nights ago. I wanted to protect what we were building. When I saw that her lights were working, I held her close, kissed her temple and promised that I would call her when I got home. Today though, I would have to step inside again. She leaned her weight onto me, bringing me back from my daydream and I glanced down to find her gazing at me the same way she had in the video. I squeezed her hand and raised the back of it to my heart before leaning down and kissing the tops of her knuckles just before the doors opened. I hoped she could feel it - my love.

The honeysuckle stems were strong and fragrant in their vase on the entryway table. She dropped her keys there and looked back at me. "They smell good, right?"

I nodded and smiled as I removed my boots. "I'm going to go fill a bag. Technically I'm not due back at the hospital until the afternoon of the 26th. Is that okay?" I rounded the corner, to greet my old friend Randolph. I'd heard her, but had forgotten to reply. She popped her head out of her bedroom and asked again, "Is that okay, Charlie?"

"It's perfect, Dr. Chris," I replied looking back in her direction.

"Can you come here for a second, Charlie?" I tried to read her tone of voice, but couldn't find any context for her beckoning me to her bedroom.

"Ummm..."

"I don't want to shout down the hallway at you."

"Okay," I slowly walked down the hallway towards her room. "Do you have clothes on?" I joked before peeking my head around the corner. "How do you change so fast, woman?" She smiled at me and shook her head. I didn't understand how she could already be in a completely different outfit than she wore home from work when we had just walked in the door. "What do you need Sugarplum?" I asked of Dr. Chris, who looked travel ready.

She grinned, "Do I need to pack anything for church or anything fancy-ish?"

"No ma'am. They'll be going to Christmas Eve service tonight," I glanced at my watch, "but we'll probably be pulling into town right as they get home from that." She nodded before turning her thoughts back to what she needed to pack. I noticed that she had moved the second carnation to her vase in here which made me smile, but her pillow was on the couch, which was a hint that she hadn't slept in her room last night. I was thinking about how I may have contributed to that which had me feeling some kind of bad.

"Charlie," I jumped, feeling like I had been caught with my hand in the cookie jar. Turning my head towards Dr. Chris, she continued, "do I need to follow you down there in my car so you can spend more time with your family?"

I smiled at her and for the first time, stepped foot in her bedroom. I walked towards her and placed my hands on her hips, looking her square in the eyes, "Thank you for asking, but we travel together, Dr.

Chris. When you need to go, we'll go."

"But I -"

"When you need to go, we will go. Mom knew there was a chance that I wasn't going to be there at all." Dr. Chris raised an eyebrow at me. I shrugged. "Don't play woman. I didn't know. I mean, I knew - I know, I just didn't -" she saved me, stopping me mid sentence, placing her index finger on my lips.

"It's okay, Charlie. My family knew I was in a holding pattern too." My eyes widened at the thought of her having a conversation with her family like I'd had with my mom. "Are you ready?"

"Can I use your bathroom before we go?" I hoped that it would give me enough time for my pulse to return to normal.

"You know where to find it!" she said before chuckling.

After returning from the bathroom, I grabbed the bag I saw her packing in the bedroom, and watched as she added fresh water to both Randolph, and the

Honeysuckle stems. She placed the pitcher on the counter near the sink, and traded it for a bag from the island counter, nodding that she was ready.

"What's in the bag?" I asked her. She pretended to zip her lips and smiled at me, ready to go. We surveyed the condo once more and I offered to help her wash our dishes before grabbing our boots and coats, and heading back to the elevator towards the parking garage and Chief. I opened the door for her and helped her inside before asking if she was in.

"I'm in, Charlie." It was the first time she had verbally responded to that question, and it stopped me in my tracks. I just stood there with her overnight bag on my left shoulder, holding the truck door open with my right hand, mulling over her face in search of an expanded answer. Her sloping smile made me go red, and there too went my heart - again. Dropping my head and tucking in my lower lip, I closed her door and placed her bag in the crew cab seat behind her. I shook my head from side to side as I walked to the driver's side and hopped in.

How did I get so lucky?

We hit the road and made sure that the truck was all fueled up before leaving Kansas City. It was a straight shot down I-49 South to my hometown, Fayetteville, Arkansas. I wouldn't consider myself the most talkative person. But the thought of being in closed quarters with Dr. Chris didn't phase me at all. In fact, I couldn't stop asking her questions. We laughed and sang our way down the road and before I knew it we were rolling into Fayetteville, and headed towards my parents' 2 story home in historic Wilson Park. I caught a glimpse of Dr. Chris as I pulled into the driveway behind my dad's truck. She looked nervous. "Hey, are you okay?"

She was taking in as much of the details as she could see in the dark; the leaf green house paint, the shingle front second story, the courtyard in front of the house, the 2nd floor balcony, the brick path that led to the front door that mom had insisted we paint red in the 90s.

"Charlie, is this where you grew up? It's beautiful!"

"Mmm hmm. Dad always makes sure that his home is a reflection of how well he takes care of his family. I've been practicing that myself."

"Charlie, those look like the honeysuckle stems that you gave me on our first date." I snickered as she continued, "They're remarkably similar! What are you laughing at?"

"I cut those from the bush in my yard that morning. That bush was grown from a clipping of this one. Mom brought it to my housewarming in Kansas City, said she was waiting until I put down roots to pass it on. Her mom, and her mom's mom, all had a piece of the bush in their yards too." She looked enamored at the thought that she was somehow wrapped up in the tradition of the winter honeysuckle.

"So who's going to be here tonight, Charlie?" she asked as I looked back to the window. We were being watched.

"Well, it looks like Mom, Dad, and maybe my," the front door swung open and out they stepped, "-grandparents." I stepped out of the truck to go open the door for Dr. Chris before my mom could beat me to it. I extended my hand for her, "You ready, Sugarplum?" I was graced with her beautiful smile again. She nodded as rapidly as she had when I asked her to come with me today. "They're going to love you." She hopped out of the truck and I grabbed her bag from the back seat. Mom met us at the fountain in the center of the courtyard and I extended my arms for a hug. She hugged Dr. Chris first instead.

"Hi sweetheart. You must be Chris!"

"I am. It's very nice to meet you Mrs. Hughes!" she replied. I shook dad's hand and gave him a hug while I overheard the woman who gave birth to me telling Dr. Chris to call her, Mom.

I turned to Dad, "Would you look at these two?" I said as he chuckled. "Merry Christmas, Mom!" I said, waiting for my hug.

"Oh, my baby," Mom said releasing her grasp on Dr. Chris. "Merry Christmas, Son!" she exclaimed before leaning in closer to my ear and whispering, "She's beautiful."

I snickered before replying, "Inside and out, Mom." She gave me a mom pat on the back before motioning for us to go inside. I reached out for Dr. Chris' hand and walked towards my parents' house with my two favorite ladies. I introduced Dr. Chris to my grandparents as we got to the porch, and they escorted us inside for a late supper before we all retired for the evening.

"Charlie, your grandparents are staying in your old room because it's bigger than the guest room." I nodded, understanding where mom was going with this. They lived in a 4 bedroom house, but one of those rooms had been converted to a dedicated office for Dad, complete with a Murphy bed. The other was mom's craft room, which meant, I was likely going to end up sleeping on the couch. There was no way they'd put the two of us in the same room. Also, I wouldn't want to make Dr. Chris uncomfortable. We'd never slept in the same bed before. "I've pulled down the Murphy bed for the two of you in your father's office."

Say what?

"There's fresh towels in there for you and fresh linens on the bed." I'd heard the words come out of her mouth, but I didn't know who this woman was that was standing in front of me. This was the same woman who created a study nook with chairs that were so far apart you had to basically yell across the room to your study partner. What on earth were we going to do about these sleeping arrangements?

"Mom, I had fully counted on camping out on the couch for a couple of nights."

"Nonsense, Son. You're good and grown now. Plus, I know you wouldn't bring a woman home and disrespect our house. Hell, this is the first time we've been lucky enough to meet someone, so I know -"

"Mom."

"Okay, Charlie. We're just so excited to have you both home for Christmas. You know where the room is."

"I do."

She reached out to hug Dr. Chris once more, kissing her on the cheek. "Goodnight sweetheart. We'll see you in the morning okay?"

"Yes ma'am. Thank you for everything. Sleep well," she replied.

What is happening here?

Feeling a bit left out, I held my own goodnight conversation, "'Goodnight Charlie. I love you, Son.' 'Oh, goodnight mom, I love you too.'"

"Goodnight Charlie," I heard mom reply as she ascended the stairs to her bedroom. I shook my head as Dr. Chris giggled.

I turned in her direction. "What's so funny ma'am?" I asked, wrapping an arm around her back and kissing her on the temple. She only shook her head. "Let me grab your bag and we'll get you settled in upstairs."

From upstairs I heard mom call down, "Charlie, I better not find you sleeping on my new couch in the morning." I shook my head and raised my arms.

"Yes ma'am," I shouted back to mom before turning to Dr. Chris and whispering, "I'll just sleep on the floor up there. It'll be fine." Dr. Chris just smiled at me as I grabbed our bags and guided her to the office bedroom. Dad had cut a few honeysuckle stems and placed them in a vase in his office.

"It smells like home, Charlie."

Chapter 2

Christmas Morning

I've performed surgeries where an incision that's off by a millimeter could be the difference between life or death, and I still can't say that I've been more nervous than I was on the drive to Charlie's childhood home. Maybe it was the fact that this was our first road trip that did it. Maybe it was the thought of meeting his parents that added another layer of nerves. I think though, that it was the thought of me stepping into my future that made my insides bubble and brew.

We'd already discussed on the phone that we both knew what this relationship was. But everything had hit the fan the day after that conversation, and I hadn't seen him since then. I thought he was gone for good, then suddenly there he was, standing in the halls of the hospital with the very thing that brought us together in the first place. We'd both gone to the coffee house with the intent of getting cider with a spoonful of sugarplums, and some outside force brought us together like two super strength magnets.

There was this pull between us, the origin of which I simply couldn't explain. Standing beside each other in awkward silence, two perfect strangers, it felt like he had wrapped me up in the safety of his arms, and yet we weren't physically touching each other at all. From that moment on, there was an ever-present warmth between us that felt like home. It was protection and love intertwined, and it was mine to be had. So, the thought that I had allowed that to slip through my fingers on Christmas Eve was torturous and excruciating to consider.

There are always pivotal moments in life that point us in one direction or another.

They shift our trajectory and change our life for better or worse. Typically I can see them clearly in hindsight. Christmas Eve though, gave me a very clear view of the shift that was happening right in front of my eyes. Add that to the list of reasons why I was so nervous. I called my mom on the way home from work to let her know that I'd be in Fayetteville, Arkansas for Christmas, and she told me that she already knew I wouldn't be celebrating with them.

"Chris, when do we get to meet Charlie?"

"Soon mom. I promise. This wasn't planned, that's for sure."

"I trust your intuition kiddo. You've always followed your gut. Be safe okay?"

"I will mom. Merry Christmas."

"Merry Christmas, Dear. I love you."

"I love you too."

————

Charlie and I took the elevator up to my condo and as each floor passed I could feel my anxiety rising. *What do I need to pack?* I made a mental note; charger, toothbrush, pajamas, two outfits. *Are they going to church tomorrow? How do I tell him that I can only stay for a day and a half? Fayetteville is almost a 4 hour drive. What are we going to do in the car for 3 and a half hours? Why does he smell so good?* I melted into him and peered up at the man I had just met a week ago, but seemingly had known my entire life. When he returned the gaze and held my hand to his heart I sensed he could feel my soul. The elevator couldn't get to R2 fast enough.

I packed as quickly as I could. We were in and out of the condo in less than 30 minutes and then it was back in the elevator on the way down to the lobby to wish Ralph a Merry Christmas, and let him know that I'd be back on the 26th. After that, it was off to Charlie's truck and onto the plowed streets of Kansas City. The trip to Fayetteville flew by, which surprised me. In fact, with the exception of that morning, most of Christmas Eve was a blur to me. That is, until we pulled into his parent's driveway that evening.

From what I could see, the exterior of

their house was charming, like something from a magazine. I soon found out that the interior was as well. But first, Charlie told me all about the family honeysuckle bush and I felt honored that he'd thought enough to include me in a tradition that spanned four generations.

As his family came outside to greet us, I felt a strong connection to his mother. Hugging her was like hugging my own mom. I don't know how much he told her about our relationship, but she hugged me like I was family that she'd known since birth. Dinner was already prepared when we arrived and it was delicious. Though I tried my hardest to, they wouldn't let me help clear the table or wash the dishes.

His mom and dad told me that washing the dishes together was part of what helped them stay connected to each other. Charlie smiled at me and dipped his head to hide his expression. He had offered to help me wash the dishes before we left my condo, but I had declined so we could get on the road and he could spend more time with his family. Now I know why he offered. My heart was in bloom.

So much of who he was came from his family. I could see bits of him in his grandparents, his mom and his dad. I didn't know it was possible, but it strengthened my love for him, and his family. Charlie didn't know it yet, but they were my family now too. He couldn't take them back if he wanted. While his parents cleaned up the kitchen and Charlie and his grandfather were engrossed in a discussion about college football, his grandmother showed me all the pictures she could find. There were some gems in there, let me tell you! I was soaking up every detail that I could. I knew my time there was limited, but I wanted to learn as much as I could about what brought them joy in life.

Just as his parents were finishing up in the kitchen, his grandparents' yawned in unison. They had been married more than 70 years, and his parents for more than 40. Together there was more than 100 years of marriage in that household. Lots of lessons to learn about how to build a relationship that lasts.

His mom, sensing their fatigue gave us an update on the sleeping arrangements. And as quickly as my nerves had settled, they came flooding back. I could feel it in my spine and down through my toes. Charlie tried his best to tell his mom that he could sleep on the couch, but she wasn't having it. So, I walked gingerly behind Charlie, the two of us slowly ascending the wooden stairwell to the 2nd floor as he led me to his dad's study turned guest room. When he opened the door, I could smell the honeysuckle stems that his dad had clipped and placed in the room. Like father, like son. They smelled exactly like the ones Charlie had gifted me on our first date.

"It smells like home, Charlie."

He turned to me and smiled, closing the door behind him.

"What are you smiling about, mister?" I asked.

"I had a dream about this." I wondered what he meant by "this." My eyebrow ticked up before I could stop it. He continued, "The first day we met, I went home that night and had a dream that I brought you home for Christmas."

"After our first date?"

He placed our bags on the floor near the window then circled in front of me, pausing to stand face to face, holding my hands in his. "No. The day you forced me into the rest of the line."

"Charlie!" I was both stunned at what he'd told me, and simultaneously felt thrown under the bus.

"What?" he smirked.

"You had a dream about me that night?"

"Several, but that's neither here nor there." He was so nonchalant in revealing this information.

"So what were the dreams about?"

"I just told you," he said, raising my arms above my head and spinning me around so he could hold me from behind without looking me in my eyes. I turned back towards him and draped my arms atop his shoulders while his arms held their position around my waist. His eyes begged for mercy.

"I won't ask you anymore questions," I

told him.

"It's not the questions. I don't mind answering them."

"What is it then?" I asked, searching his eyes for an honest reply.

"You can't stand this close to me, woman," he said as a smile tipped the corners of his mouth.

I grinned as I softly whispered near his ear, "Why not, Charlie?"

He lowered his forehead to mine and spoke tenderly in hushed tones, "You're gonna get me grounded."

That was the last thing I remembered before he kissed me. I'm certain some other words exited my mouth before our lips met, but they seemed so insignificant compared to the feeling of standing smack in the middle of the swirl of emotions associated with kissing Charlie. He was home and I suddenly had an overwhelming desire to ensure that he knew I'd take good care of him. I'm sure it confused him when he realized that I had a trail of tears streaking down the left side of my face. He didn't say a single word, just wiped them away and held me lovingly in his arms. It almost felt like he was safeguarding my heart. *Stethoscope.*

This time there were no cell phones to interrupt the moment. No elevator doors to contend with. Just Charlie and I and the still of the night, until the quiet knock on the door. He was still holding me in his arms when he told whomever was on the other side to come in. His dad peeked his head inside, "Goodnight you two."

"Goodnight Dad," Charlie replied.

"Y'all need anything, you know where to find it. Chris, if you don't know where to find it, wake Charlie up. He'll get it for you."

"Yes, sir," I said through a slight chuckle - still wrapped in Charlie's embrace.

Turning his attention back towards his only son, who rested his cheek atop my head, "Don't get grounded now, Charlie."

"We'll see, Dad," he laughed.

His dad snickered, "We'll see? Mary's in labor, walking around town lookin' for room at the inn right now. Tonight is the night Jesus was born. Y'all can wait a day."

"I won't let him get grounded, Mr. Hughes," I offered.

"You better not, Chris. You're family now. We'll ground you too, Daughter," he said with an ornery smile. Charlie squeezed me tighter. "Sleep well children."

"You too, Dad," we said in unison. His dad closed the door and we listened to his footsteps trailing down the hallway.

"I told you they'd love you," Charlie said to me with a quick kiss to my temple. "Let me show you where the bathroom is so you can change clothes and handle whatever other business you need to handle."

I grabbed my bag of toiletries and pajamas and followed Charlie down the hallway to the bathroom. He left me at the doorway and asked for a few minutes so he could change clothes. I figured by the time I emptied my bladder, changed clothes and brushed my teeth that should be plenty of time for him to change.

I tiptoed down the hallway back to the room, trying not to disturb any sleeping parents or grands and I caught a glimpse of Charlie's mom on the main level, stuffing presents underneath their fresh cut Christmas tree. I didn't knock on the door to the office so I wouldn't startle his mom. Instead I startled a shirtless Charlie, who had to be the slowest changing man in the entire world. I raised a finger to my lips so he wouldn't make too much noise. "Your mom is downstairs playing Santa."

He scrambled to throw on his t-shirt, "She hasn't done that in years, Chris."

"I just saw her. That's why I didn't knock to let you know I was coming in." We heard her footsteps heading back down the hallway to her bedroom and Charlie waited until their door closed before he slipped out to brush his teeth.

I surveyed the room. Charlie had been setting up his makeshift sleeping arrangements. That must have been why he hadn't finished changing yet. He'd moved a pillow from the Murphy bed, down to the hardwood floor, along with a thin quilt. There was no way I was letting him sleep on the floor. I knew he would try to stop me if I asked him to sleep in the bed, so I remade it, creating two distinct sleeping sections for us. When he returned, I was sitting in his dad's office chair, waiting for him to let me know if he had a side of the bed that he preferred to sleep on, because I didn't. He shook his head at me and led me to the bed, tucking me in and kissing me on the temple before turning off the lights and walking to the other side of the bed.

"Goodnight, Charlie."

"Goodnight, Beautiful."

It was the best night's sleep I'd had in a long time. I didn't fall asleep worrying about a patient, or concerned about the mounting list of items on my to do list. None of those thoughts were around. Instead I went to sleep surrounded by a feeling of safety and love. I was tremendously appreciative of the grace I had received. What a day!

I awoke the next morning knowing that Charlie would be in the bed beside me, wrapped underneath his own set of sheets and quilt, but he wasn't there. His pillow was still there, so I knew he hadn't crept onto the floor in the middle of the night. But he himself was gone. I reached for my glasses, and peered towards the door, where I noticed it was left slightly cracked open. I lay as still as possible, listening to see if everything was okay. The clock on the wall read 7:30, so I knew it was still morning, unlike the last time I fell asleep in his arms and it was already after noon when we woke up.

I heard him in the hallway, trying to be quiet, "I think she's still sleep, Grandma."

"It's Christmas morning, Charlie!"

I could hear the echo of his shortened gate inching down the hallway as quietly as possible. I couldn't help but smile as he tried his best to quietly open the creaky door to his dad's office and peek inside to see if I was still sleep.

He beamed as he spoke in a near whisper, "Hey! Good morning, Dr. Chris! Merry Christmas!"

Suddenly unsure of how to greet him,

I waved in his direction and rolled onto my side to face him, "Merry Christmas, Charlie! Is everything okay?"

He grinned wide enough for me to see both sets of teeth, "Mm hmm. Did you sleep well?"

I nodded in slow motion, my words following the rhythm of my head, "Best sleep ever. Did you?"

His grin closed as he shook his head no. "I was too busy worrying that I would instinctively reach out for you in the middle of the night."

His answer froze me, "Oh!"

"Yeah, it was rough," he said as he ran his hand over the back of his head, smoothing his hair into place.

I could see the fatigue in his eyes, "Are you going to be okay?"

He touched his hand to his heart, looking away for a split second, "Oh yeah, I'll be fine. Hey, Grandma has fixed Christmas breakfast for everyone. She's waking up Grandpa and my parents. Don't try to change,we eat it in our pajamas.”

I nodded, “There’s no way I can say no to your grandma.” Charlie smiled at me and extended a hand to help me out of bed. “But I probably need to make a pit stop before I head downstairs for breakfast.”

After a brief detour to the bathroom, I found my way down to the kitchen where everyone was seated except for Charlie’s grandpa. Charlie stood to help me in with my seat while his grandma called up to her husband, who we could faintly hear vocalizing his way down the hallway, “Little Christmas tree, no one to buy you…” Charlie’s grandpa lumbered down the wooden steps as quickly as he could, singing all the way down. I took a quick glance at Charlie, who raised his eyebrows and patted my knee underneath the table.

“Good morning, good morning!! Merry Christmas one and all!” he exclaimed, waving to everyone like he was in a parade. He plopped down in his seat and commented on the delicious smell of the Christmas breakfast spread in front of us.

“It does smell delicious,” Charlie’s dad

commented. "I bet it tastes just as good as it smells, Dad!"

"Well we'd better get to blessing this food then, I suppose, huh?" his grandfather replied before bowing his head and proceeding to pray. "Dear Heavenly Father, we thank you for this special day in which we gather to celebrate your love for us, sent through your son, Jesus Christ. May we continue to keep him in the center of all things we do and reflect his love in our service to others. We thank you for safe keeping and bringing Charlie and his bride, Chris home to celebrate with us this year." I felt Charlie and his dad both squeeze my hand. "We are grateful for time spent together and the memories we'll create and keep throughout the years to come. We thank you for the food we are about to receive and we humbly ask that you also look kindly upon those in need. These things we pray in Jesus name, Amen."

And the table said, "Amen."

Slightly afraid to move, I waited a heartbeat or two before looking at Charlie, who mouthed an apology to me. I shrugged my shoulders and caught a glimpse of his mom, admiring the two of us from across the table. We all began to fill our plates and pass the food in silence before, Charlie's grandmother spoke, "You know they're not married yet, right Charles?"

"I mean they haven't had a ceremony yet, Elizabeth, but look at the boy's face!" I tried to suppress my smile, though I couldn't help but laugh as he finished speaking, "If he's not in love, I don't know what love looks like. Are you telling me I don't know what love looks like?"

"That's not what I'm telling you at all, Dear," she said with a slight shake of the head.

"Well alright then! We get to spend Christmas with our grandson," he paused for dramatic effect, "and his bride. She doesn't have to be married yet to be a bride, does she?"

Charlie sharply turned his head towards his grandfather's chair, "Grandpa!"

"Oh hush boy. Have you ever brought a woman to this house with you? And on Christmas?"

"No sir, but -"

"Are you going to marry her?"

"I mean we haven't talked about," Charlie paused and looked at me, his head cocked to the side, as he passed me the plate of sausage and bacon. "Well, I guess we did talk about it already," he said, surprised at his own answer.

His grandfather nodded his head in confirmation. "Mm hmm. You love her. You've talked about it. She's your bride. Let's eat!"

Charlie opened his mouth to speak but wasn't fast enough. "Amen!" his dad replied, as I passed the plate of breakfast meat to him. Charlie sat stunned, poking his fork at his pancakes. I patted him on the knee underneath the table to let him know that things were okay and that nothing had changed, but I wasn't sure this conversation didn't jar him. His sheepish smile told me that everything would be okay - he was just a little embarrassed.

The rest of the breakfast was far less eventful than the beginning of it. His family all had questions about my family's Christmas traditions. I told them about us attending morning church service before we returned for Christmas brunch and opening presents, and that we celebrated with the extended family over a Christmas dinner that finished with harmonious carols sung by all members of our family. As I spoke, I could feel myself beginning to think about all that I was missing by being here with Charlie and I could feel a lump growing in my throat.

"Well, we are certainly grateful that your family shared you with us this year," his mom offered, sensing my distress. "Is there anyway for you to see them today? Can you video chat with them?"

"I bet we can," I responded, feeling slightly more at ease about what I was missing.

After breakfast I excused myself to go grab my phone before returning downstairs. I sent my sister a text to see when she and the kids would be visiting our parents' house and asked if they'd like to get in a bit of face time before heading to see the extended family.

"You don't want us to pass the phone around at dinner so all your aunts, uncles and crazy cousins can meet Charlie?"

"Girl no. Not yet."

Speaking to Charlie's mom, I asked if 1:30 would be okay and told her that everyone would like to meet them.

"Certainly! We should be out of our pajamas by then," she laughed.

I confirmed the time with my sister then helped clear the table. I also tried my best to help wash the dishes before getting shooed out of the kitchen again. Charlie, had moved into the family room and plopped down on the couch near his grandma.

"You know your grandfather was just teasing you, right Charlie?" she said, patting him on his hand.

He nodded in reply, "I know, grandma. He just put us in an awkward spot, that's all."

"I think Chris is okay, Charlie. She seemed to take it all in stride. You know, your mother called me as soon as she got off the phone with you a few days ago."

"She did?"

"Mm hmm. She told me that you sounded different on the phone."

"How so, Grandma?" he asked, attempting to stifle a smile.

"Well, you'll have to ask your mother about that, but I know she told me that if you could make it home for Christmas that you would be bringing Chris with you."

"I didn't even tell her that I was going to ask her to come with me, Grandma."

"You didn't have to tell her Charlie. Moms just know sometimes."
"What else did she tell you?"

"That you cared deeply for her, that you took care of her the same way your father did when he first met your mother."

I didn't mean to be eavesdropping on their conversation. I just kind of unexpectedly lumbered into the outskirts of the room while they were in the middle of a conversation that just so happened to be partially about me. I didn't know what to do. I didn't want to startle them, but if I left the room, I was certain to make a noise or two. So I stood still while their conversation continued. Charlie's grandpa saved me, walking up beside me and squeezing my elbow to get me to walk with him, pretending that we had been in a conversation with each other as we walked into the family room together. This family was full of kind hearts like Charlie and I loved every single one of them.

His grandma was wrapping up their conversation as his grandfather and I took a seat, him in the chair beside his wife, and I beside Charlie on the couch. "That's how she knew, Charlie."

"That's how who knew what, Elizabeth?" Grandpa Charles inserted. She looked at him like he was the most ornery person in the world.

"It's Christmas, be kind," he laughed.

Charlie smiled at the two of them as they reached across the arms of their respective chairs to hold hands with each other. He opened his palm towards me, just as he had on our first date. I placed my hand in his and relaxed into his shoulder just as he intertwined his fingers with mine. His grandparents looked lovingly in our direction and shared an inside joke with each other before starting an epic story.

"Do you remember our first Christmas together, Elizabeth?"

"I do, Charles," she remembered fondly.

Grandpa Charles spoke, directing his story towards me, "I had just met her a few days before Christmas, Chris. We had only gone on two dates, but I knew the moment I saw her that I was going to be her husband. When that Christmas arrived, I showed up on her doorstep with a bow," he was so tickled that he couldn't finish his story.

"My father answered the door, and there was this cocky young man, standing on the porch, holding a bow in his hands, and asking if he could speak with me. We were so young. I was in senior high school and daddy wasn't having any of that. He just closed the door on him. Didn't say a word."

She shook her head and laughed as the scene replayed in her mind. "So my mother comes rushing to the door, stammering something about it being Christmas Day and Daddy needing to be more Christ-like in his walk, especially today. So my father turns back around and opens the door."

Charlie's grandfather laughed so hard it brought him to tears. His grandmother patted his hand as she tried to finish the story. "So daddy turns back around and opens the door and says, 'Merry Christmas, young man. How can I help you?' and this guy here opened his mouth and asks to speak with my Daddy man to man. Well daddy told him, 'You gotta be a man to have a man-to-man talk, son,' and closed the door again. Momma stared at him hard enough to cut a hole through his head, so he turned around and opened the door again."

I giggled at the thought of it. "Where were you as all this happened," I asked her.

"I was watching from the top of the stairs, afraid to move an inch." She chuckled some more and continued, "So Daddy opened the door again and Charles immediately started reciting the poem, "Still Here" by

Langston Hughes. Daddy laughed so hard he extended a hand for him to come inside and said, 'What's your name son?' Charlie, your grandfather looked at your great grandfather and told him that his name was Sonnin Law. Momma snickered as Daddy turned towards the stairs and hollered - he didn't know I was watching from the top of the stairs, see - 'Elizabeth, Sonnin Law is here to see you!'"

We were all in tears of laughter by that point in the story.

"So I said, 'Who, sir?' and he turned back towards Charles to see if he had pronounced it correctly. Charles nodded. Momma's laughing. Daddy repeats himself, 'Sonnin Law! Just come down here so you can say hello.' So I saunter down the steps, nervous as I don't know what, and there's Charles, bow in hand, waiting for me to reach the bottom step. He slips it on my wrist and says to me..."

Grandpa Charles got it together just enough to recite it with her, "Merry Christmas my dearest Elizabeth. You would make this the best Christmas on record if you would allow me to be your husband."

"Daddy grabbed him by the collar and said, 'Hold on there sonny boy, nobody called you son in law!' Then momma stepped in. 'Well now hold on. You just did dear. You're Charles Hughes, right?' Charles, politely agreed with momma and looked back to me. I turned back towards Daddy, who stood in stunned silence at the trickery."

"Her mom wished me a Merry Christmas and invited me to stay for dinner, and we've spent every Christmas together since that first year. No matter where I was or where work took me, I always made it home to her for Christmas."

Charlie's parents came in just at the tail end of the story. "Was this the story about how you asked mom to marry you, Dad?" They nodded.

Sounding somewhat shocked by his own admission, Grandpa Charles shared, "We've spent more than 70 Christmases together Chris. Can you believe that?"

It was definitely impressive.

His mom turned towards me, "Has

Charlie told you about how his father and I met yet?"

"Not yet!" I replied, eager to hear more.

"No, don't tell her that story!" Charlie said, sounding slightly embarrassed.

His dad started to tell me all about this blind date that went completely left, and how he was trying to find a way to exit gracefully and without leaving the woman stranded.

"The entire night that we were in the restaurant, I kept locking eyes with this woman who was sitting with her friends. She was stunning, but I knew I'd look like a jerk for flirting with someone while I was on a date with another woman - even if my date was shouting across the restaurant at the wait staff from our table. At some point I had excused myself to go to the bathroom. I just needed a break from all that energy! When I came back, my date was gone, and sitting at the table was the stunning woman who was making eyes at me all night. So I said, 'Excuse me miss. I think you might be at the wrong table.' She told me to have a seat and play along if I wanted to get out of my date. I sat down as fast as I could and introduced myself. She nodded. I could feel this warm energy between us, and tried my hardest not to let it distract me."

I nodded, understanding the energy he was describing.

"So my date begins her return to the table. We could hear her coming the moment she left the ladies' room. She's shouting, 'Who's this sitting at the table with my man? I don't know what you think is going on hunny, but he and I are on a date.' Stunning woman looks at my date, and back at me, then at my date, then back at me and says, 'Is this her, Charles? Is this the woman that took you away from your family, from your wife and 4 children, and at Christmas?' I'm shocked, but I play along because that date was the worst 45 minutes of my entire young life. So I start stuttering, pretending like I'm caught in a trap. 'FOUR CHILDREN!' my date shouted. The entire restaurant turned their attention in our direction. My date stormed out of the restaurant mumbling something about not being caught in the middle of a shit show. She was the show. So I stand and take a bow, then grab the hand of my stunning leading lady, and point to her. She curtsied and the restaurant goers cheered."

"Oh wow!" I said, completely engrossed in the story.

"The moment I held her hand, I knew that I was going to marry her," he finished, looking over at his wife.

Charlie's mom spoke up, "She was a mess, Chris and he looked so miserable sitting over there with her."

"I was miserable!" he joked.

"So what happened after you took a bow?" I asked with bated breath. I slowly exhaled with each word that flowed from his mom's mouth.

"He paid for dinner for my friends and I, thanked me for saving him, and left the restaurant." I looked at Charlie's dad, who was shaking his head in shame.

"I spent 3 whole weeks trying to find her again," he laughed. "I call myself visiting every restaurant and bar in town. I even took slow strolls by all the beauty shops so

I could peek in the windows in search of her. I did see her once though."

"No you didn't," his mom replied.

"Yes I did. I saw her one time with a guy I went to high school with. He had brought her flowers and was wooing her."

"That wasn't me, Charles!"

"I know, but I thought it was you, and I had all but given up hope of finding you. Then a friend of mine came home on leave from the army and needed a friend to go on a double first date with him."

"Was she your date?" I asked, hopeful that he'd found her that way.

"No," he laughed. "She was HIS date!" Charlie's mom verified his story with a nod.

"Oh my!" I laughed.

"Oh my, indeed!" he said.

"So what did you do?" I asked, eager to hear the rest of the story.

"Don't tell her, Dad," Charlie begged, placing his head in his hands.

"I caught her eye and flashed a quick smile and she knew what to do. So I opened my mouth to speak just as he was about to introduce me to my date. I said, 'Is this him? Is this the guy you left me for, Linda?' He said, 'Linda? I thought you said your name was Lois!' So I asked her, 'Him or Me?' I said, 'I need you to choose right now.'" At this point in the story I'm sure a fly would have found a good home in my mouth. It was wide open in disbelief. "She gazed into my eyes and extended a hand for me before stoically speaking, 'Charles, it's always been you. It will always be you.' Before I knew it we were on our way to the Justice of the Peace to get married.

"Just like that?" I asked.

"Just like that," they both replied.

Charlie's mom continued, "Things were different in the late 60s and early 70s. The Vietnam War was still going on, and people were being drafted left and right. We didn't know what secrets tomorrow held, so we lived largely in the moment." I nodded, understanding what she was saying.

"She's always been my warrior, protecting our space and home. Best decision I ever made was to go on that blind date with the crazy lady. I was saved by Lois' love," Mr. Hughes shared.

"Right after we got married, I got sick. So sick, they didn't think I was going to make it. Charles was right there taking care of me each and every day. My organs started to fail, but he fought so hard for me to stay that I fought too. My body had gone through a battle, but I survived. We actually were told that it would be too risky for me to have children, and we never thought that we'd have any kids at all, so when we found out that I was carrying Charlie, we loved him instantly."

"I was perfectly content just spending the rest of my life with her, as God saw fit for her to stay just a little bit longer with us. We could have adopted, or fostered children, it didn't matter. I was just elated to spend the rest of my time with her because I had already experienced the thought of losing her, and that just wasn't something I was prepared to handle after we ditched the double daters and ran off to get married. Then this knucklehead came into the picture when I needed to grow as a man, and here we are. I'm so proud of who he is."

I was in tears by this point and Charlie rubbed my shoulder to comfort me. I turned my head around to find him wiping away a tear or two of his own. I patted his knee again and let my hand rest in place. He laced his fingers between mine and lifted my hand to his lips, just as he had done in the elevator in the condo, yesterday.

Grandma Elizabeth chimed in, "So, that's why we're so excited to expand the family, Chris. We've watched him figure out and build his professional life, and know that he'll only continue to grow into a stronger human being with the right support by his side."

"Look at how he's looking at his bride!" Grandpa Charles joked.

"If he loves you, we love you without question," his mom replied.

I could only muster two words, "Thank you."

"Okay, enough, enough!" his dad chided. "Are we getting dressed before or after exchanging gifts?" As a family they voted to open gifts afterwards and we all returned to our rooms to get cleaned up. With a bathroom attached to both Charlie's old room, and his parent's master bedroom, we had the hallway bathroom to ourselves to share. Problem was, we had to leave the room to get cleaned up. He was so overcome with emotion, that I could hardly get the door closed before he started speaking his mind, and the words seemed to flow from him with a fury and passion like I've never seen before.

"Chris, thank you for sharing Christmas day with my family."

"Thank you for sharing your family with me, Charlie."

He sat down on the end of the Murphy Bed and guided me to stand in front of him as he lightly held my fingers in his. His gaze was intense. "They were right when they said I've never brought anyone home to meet them. I haven't. Not even in high school. I didn't understand those 'how we met' stories until today. It didn't make sense to me how they could just instinctively know that they had met their person because I hadn't met mine until two weeks ago, which sounds absolutely ridiculous to say out loud. I loved you before I knew you, which is how I can know for certain that I love you right now."

My heart was full. It was the first time I'd heard him speak those words and I was taking a mental snapshot of the moment so I'd remember all the details, right down to the twinkle in his eyes. I leaned down to kiss him and he stopped me, placing two fingers on my lips.

"Don't start that while I'm sitting on the bed. You're gonna get me grounded."

"Hmm. Probably so," I said, watching him fight through whatever internal desire was brewing inside of him. I backed away from him, letting go of his grasp and turning my attention to the clothes I was going to wear after taking a shower. Charlie fell backwards on the bed and rested with his hands over his heart. He looked as though a weight had been lifted from his shoulders.

"You okay?" I asked.

His head rolled in my direction. "Oh

yeah, I'm great," he said, a broad smile stretched across his face. Right there in that moment, it occurred to me that this love that I was experiencing didn't look anything like the slow build up I had envisioned. Instead it rolled in on a wave and crashed down upon me, drenching me with its presence and filling every crevice it could find its way into, before carving a path straight to my heart.

"Charlie?" I called out to him.

"Yes, Sugarplum?" he asked, still smiling ear to ear.

I smiled back at him, knowing that I couldn't take back the words I was about to say, nor would I want to even if I could, "I love you deeply."

"Stethoscope," he laughed before closing his eyes and shaking his head.

Chapter 3

Christmas Afternoon

Charlie:

She said the words I didn't even realize I was waiting to hear before grabbing her clothes to head to the shower. As she was getting cleaned up, I dropped to my knees and began to say a quick prayer to God for sending me to the coffee shop to seek resolution when he did. I promised him that I would take good care of Dr. Chris. She was truly the woman I didn't know I needed, and a blessing I wasn't sure I deserved. Once she returned from getting cleaned up, I took my turn in the bathroom. I showered as quickly as I could so I wouldn't miss the video chat with her family.

We gathered around Thomas, the Christmas tree exchanging gifts. That was the name my mother had chosen for their first Christmas Tree, and subsequently every Christmas Tree that followed.

We watched as each person opened one gift at a time, taking in the moment. Dr. Chris wasn't expecting anything, but I knew my mom was going to take care of her as soon as she invited her to join us for Christmas during our last phone call. When she handed the small box to her, Dr. Chris looked confused. She grabbed the other bag she had brought with her, and pulled out four boxes, one the same size as the box mom had handed to her. Returning to the floor beside me, Dr. Chris handed the small box to mom, then one each of the other three boxes to my grandparents, my dad, and then me.

"You didn't have to get us anything Chris," Mom told Dr. Chris.

"I wanted to gift you something meaningful," she told her in return.

I leaned closer to her ear and whispered, "When did you have the chance to get them something? I was with you most of the day yesterday." She simply smiled and winked at me.

Dr. Chris and mom opened their gifts at the same time and started laughing. Without showing anyone else what it was, they stood to their feet and hugged each other before mom kissed her on the cheek. Dad looked at me to see if I knew what she'd gotten her and I shrugged.

"Oh gracious," Mom said, seemingly flabbergasted by the gift she had been given.

"Well what was it, Lois?" Dad asked.

They stopped hugging long enough to hold up the same heart shaped locket etched with a vine outline and a message that read, "Love Grows Here."

Dr. Chris sat back down beside me on the floor and leaned in to whisper a message to me. "After our first date, I ordered that to give to your mom the first time I met her." Just when I didn't think I could love her any more, she surprised me. I kissed her temple and watched as my grandparents and dad opened their gifts from Dr. Chris.

"Are these Sugarplums?" Grandma Lois asked.

"They are!" she exclaimed.

"Did you make these?" Grandma continued.

"I did. You'll have to ask Charlie about their significance," Dr. Chris finished.

I told them all about the story of how we met the first time, which spurred questions about how we met the second time around. Thankfully we were spared by Dr. Chris' sister, who was dialing in for their video chat.

Dr. Chris & her sister, Yvonne, look so much alike. In her condo, there's a picture of the two of them when they were little girls, but I hadn't seen an adult version of her older sister yet. To see them together was like nearly looking at twins. I watched from over her shoulder until I heard the question, "So where is Charlie?" I leaned in close to Dr. Chris and waved hello to her sister.

"Hey Charlie!" Vonne, said with a familiar elated smile. "You're a handsome one, aren't you?"

"Vonne!" Dr. Chris said.

"Am I lying, Chris?" she asked in a way that only a big sister can do. Dr. Chris patted my cheek and shook her head no. "Are you taking good care of my sister down there?"

"Always," I replied without thinking about my answer.

"Oh, always huh?" Vonne replied, while chuckling. In the distance, I heard a voice that I imagined is what Dr. Chris would eventually sound like as she got older.

"Is that Charlie?" a voice asked of Vonne, who told the voice to come over and say hello.

"Hi Charlie! Oh, he's a looker!" I imagined my cheeks were probably a little rosy.

"Hi Mom! Merry Christmas to you too!"

"Merry Christmas, Chris!" she replied laughing.

"Mom, this is Charlie. Charlie, this is my mom."

"Hi Mrs. James! It's nice to meet you. Hopefully we'll meet in person soon."

"Call me Mom, sweetheart," she said to me before turning to Vonne and saying, "Look at Chris' face, Vonne. She's in love with him." My parents and grandparents chuckled.

A bit embarrassed by her mom's presumed off-the-record remark, Dr. Chris quickly chimed in, "Mom. Hey Mom, we can hear you."

"You heard what I said to Vonne?" she asked her daughter.

"We all did, Mom," Dr. Chris replied. I nodded.

"Well, now I know!" she chuckled. "Chris, let me talk to Charlie."

"He's right here mom."

"I know that. I can see him. I can also see you. I just want to talk to Charlie for a minute." Dr. Chris nodded in reply to her mom's comment and handed the phone to me before sliding out of frame. "Is she gone?" her mom asked.

"Yes ma'am," I respectfully replied while trying not to look at Dr. Chris from the corner of my eye.

"Charlie, that's my baby girl. You'll take good care of her won't you?"

"Yes ma'am."

"She keeps her feelings close to her heart. So if she ever gets to a place where she feels comfortable telling you that she loves you, know that she wholeheartedly means it." I nodded and listened some more. "She's never spent Christmas away from us without being at the hospital, I mean with another family, you know. So I know she must care a lot about you."

I smiled, hearing her mom spill the beans about her daughter. "She does. I can feel it. I feel the same way about her."

"Mmm hmm. I can see that. It's written all over your face and the way you look at her. Have you told her how you feel about her?"

"Yes ma'am, I have," I said grinning as I thought about this morning and the look on Dr. Chris' face as I finally spoke those words aloud.

"Yes you have, Charlie. Look at that smile!" I laughed as she continued. "I know that will help her to trust again. Would you like to chat with her dad?" she asked passing the phone to Dr. Chris' father before I had the chance to answer.

"Oh, who is this I'm looking at?" he asked his wife.

"That's Charlie, baby," she said, patting him.

"Do I know Charlie?" he asked, peering over the top of his eyeglasses.

"Not yet," she told him emphatically.

"Oh. So, why am I talking to Charlie?"

Dr. Chris leaned into view, "Hi Dad!"

"Hey baby-girl! Oh, this is ChARlie!" Dr. Chris nodded and leaned out of the way.

"Well, hello, Charlie!"

"Hi sir. Merry Christmas!"

"Merry Christmas to you too! How's the weather where you are?"

"It's about 45 degrees and a little cloudy here. How about there in Kansas City?"

"Well, it's trying to snow here again. I'm hoping that it holds off though. When are you two supposed to head back this way?"

"First thing tomorrow morning," I told him.

"Dear? What's the forecast here for tomorrow morning?"

From a distance, Dr. Chris' mom shouted, "More snow!"

"More snow here tomorrow it sounds like. You two be careful on the road okay?"

"Yes sir."

"Okay now, where'd my daughter go?"

Dr. Chris leaned back into frame and spoke up, "I'm right here Dad."

I handed the phone back to Dr. Chris just as he started to ask her another question, "You staying safe in Arkansas?"

"Yes. The Hughes family is taking good care of me, Dad," she said with a smile.

"Are they nearby too? Can I say hello?"

"Sure! she said, turning the phone around to show him everyone in the room. "Who would you like to speak with first?"

"Whomever is closest! I just want to say hello."

As Dr. Chris handed the phone to my parents, I could hear her dad calling to her mom. "Cille? Lucille? Come here and say hello to Charlie's family!"

My mom waited to turn the phone around to face them until she saw Dr. Chris'

Mom. Then the four of them started waving and saying hello like they were long lost family members who were reuniting after 50 years.

"It's so good to meet you!"

"How are you?"

"Wow, she looks just like you."

"He sure is a good mix of the two of you." I wasn't sure who was saying what. It was all so jumbled and mixed in there together.

"Thank you for taking care of our daughter!" her mom offered, getting choked up.

"It's our pleasure having her here with us. She has such a beautiful spirit," my mom said. I couldn't have agreed more.

Dr. Chris and I sat on the couch and watched our parents laugh and joke with each other about what it must be like to date now and how happy they were that we found our way to each other. She turned her head and smiled in my direction and leaned into my shoulder nook. I felt an overwhelming sense of peace consume me as I rested my cheek upon the top of her head and we continued to watch the current episode of Christmas Chronicles happening in my parents house as my grandparents joined the conversation.

They traded stories about our childhoods and some of the stubborn streaks we showed as children, which led them to know we would be strong adults. I was grateful that our stubbornness didn't take over and prevent this day from existing in the continuum of time. Speaking of, our parents had no concept of time, I wondered if that was part of the beauty of retirement. Either way, they carried on so much that they didn't seem to notice as we slipped up to the second floor balcony overlooking the backyard to sneak in a private moment with each other.

———

She was enthralled by the view of the city and mentioned something about how fresh the air was. I was too busy checking out what was in my own range of vision to notice that of the city. We looked out upon the treetops in silence, standing in the comfort of each other's presence. I tried to stay present, I really did. But before I knew it, I was daydreaming about the two of us bringing our children here to visit their grandparents. I never saw myself as a dad, but I did see myself as the best uncle & godfather possible. Suddenly, all of that was different. I wanted a family. I wanted to raise a family, but with Dr. Chris. I was changing. Thank, God, I was changing.

"Charlie, did you spend a lot of time up here when you were younger?"

"Not really. The view wasn't as beautiful as it is now." She looked at me, eyes full of endearment.

"Hey sir, don't get yourself grounded now."

"How about you don't get yourself grounded. I see how you're looking at me. You heard my dad!"

"I did."

"You willing to risk it?" I asked jokingly.

"I'm considering my options," she said with a sly smile.

"No ma'am. Let's get you back inside!"

"You go ahead, Charlie. I want to have a talk with God."

I nodded in respect, "Tell Him I said hello."

She smiled but her body language told me that it was going to be a serious talk.

———

Dr. Chris:
Would I have imagined this would have been my life two weeks ago? Absolutely not. I was overflowing with gratitude and needed to speak my mind to the universe. Lifting my face towards the sky I acknowledged all that I was feeling; the good, the challenging, the overwhelmingly positive. Each and every single thing that entered my mind, I welcomed, as it had all led me to this point. I spoke of my gratefulness in the abundance of love that had entered my life; Charlie's grandparents, his parents, Charlie himself. I was forming

a second family and I asked that He help me not overthink anything. I asked for guidance in keeping my heart at the center of our conversations. I requested the ability to stay in the moment. Love wasn't easy for me in the past, but Charlie gave me hope that I could trust him. I asked that I always be able to see that his actions for what they were in spite of my filter and that I find the tools necessary to sustain a long term relationship. With one final thank you, I turned around to go find Charlie, only to see him rising from his knees and a prayer of his own. He looked in my direction to see if I was still going or if I had finished. Sensing that I was done, he joined me back out on the balcony, reaching for my hand.

"Everything okay?" I asked him.

"All good here. Everything okay with you?"

"Everything's good here us well," I replied.

"Should we go see what our parents are talking about now?" he asked. I laughed. He finished his thought, "'cause you know they're not done talking."

"They're definitely not done talking."

"Should we take them a charger?"

"Probably so. But-"

"What's up?" he asked. I hesitated, and the pitch of his voice lead me to think he thought that something was wrong. "What is it Chris?"

"I was thinking, you know about what I said earlier."

"I love you deeply?"

"Mmm hmmm. Yeah," I said pausing again.

"What is it Chris?" he asked, his face full of concern.

"I just want you to know that I wasn't saying it in reply to what you said to me. I need you to know that I really meant it."

"I can feel it. I know you meant it," he said as he rubbed my coat covered back with his gloved hand. "...and I love you deeply too," he said before kissing my temple.

"Stethoscope."

He chuckled and reeled me backwards into his arms as we stared out into space. I was most definitely at home. We stood outside for at least 10 minutes, watching the world pass us by when it suddenly occurred to me that we probably needed to get downstairs to be with our parents. Who knew what our unsupervised family would discuss next?

"We probably need to go deliver that charging cord, Charlie."

"Mmm hmm," he said as he gathered and lifted my hair from my neck, bent my coat collar down, and kissed me on the nape of my neck. It was a simple peck that sent complex shock waves down my spine and rooted me to the balcony floor through the soles of my feet. He leaned away from me, "Let's go, Dr. Chris."

"Go where, Charlie?" I asked him. He chuckled and spun me around.

"To give them the charger so we can buy some time and not get grounded..."

"Would they really ground us, Charlie?"

"I'm not tempting fate. I used to live here," he said.

I raised my heels off the balcony and caressed the side of his face with the back of my hand, running my fingertips over the outline of his beard, before turning my attention to his ears. "No, woman. Leave my ears alone," he joked. His dad, cleared his throat as he stepped into the room adjacent to the balcony.

"Pardon me, lovebirds. Hope I'm not interrupting anything! Do you have a charging cable for your phone, Chris?"

"I do. I'll go grab it for you," I said, leaving Charlie with his dad.

I was only gone for a moment, but when I returned to the balcony, the two of them were yucking it up like they had been fully engrossed in a deep conversation. Charlie's Dad patted his son on the back before I interrupted their father-son bonding time, "Here's that cable and charging block, Mr. Hughes."

"Don't forget what I told you, son," he said turning in my direction and politely receiving the charging cord from me. "Thank you, Daughter."

"You're welcome, Dad," I said with a smile.

"There we go. That's more like it. We'll see you downstairs in a bit."

"You bet!" I said. And with that, he left us alone to our own devices again.

Charlie and I somehow found our way back to each others' intertwined limbs. We took a seat on the gliding bench on the balcony and I sidled up beside him. It was hard not to find myself wrapped up in his comforting arms. He was such a doting partner. As needy and clingy as it seemed, I felt like couldn't get close enough to him. "Charlie, I feel so safe in your arms."

"Yeah?" he asked softly. I nodded quietly in reply and focused on the soothing motion of the bench. "Dr. Chris, what were you thinking about when we were staring out over the treetops?"

I wasn't sure how much to tell him. There were so many things that crossed my mind. "You first, Charlie."

He laughed nervously and stalled, "Well..."

I gave the conversation a bit of space to breathe before speaking. "I'm listening..."

He took a breath and spilled his thoughts. "I was trying to stay in the moment, so I thought about the scent of your hair, then the feel of your hands and the way you felt in my arms, a little bit about how content I was, and of course about the way you get along with my family. Then my thoughts drifted."

"Where did they drift to, Charlie?"

Laughing nervously he replied, "I've answered the question, right?"

"I mean partially."

"What's missing?" he asked with a laugh.

A smirk danced across my face, "The

rest of your thoughts.”

“I'll give you the rest after you tell me what you were thinking about,” he said nuzzling his nose on my cheek before gracing it with a quick peck.

I blurted out my thoughts and tried to shift the focus back to him as fast as possible. “I was thinking about what my future family would look like. Okay, I'm ready for the rest of your thoughts.”

“Wow.”

“What?” I nervously asked.

Save for the rhythmic squeak of the glider, silence filled the balcony. I couldn't tell how he felt about my statement.

“Those were the rest of my future thoughts.”

I looked at him gingerly, “You didn't say anything.”

“No. What you said is what I was thinking about.”

“A future family?”

"Yes. Well, more specifically our family and bringing children back here to visit their grandparents."

"How many children did you see, Charlie?"

"Three."

"Me too."

In unison, we shared, "Two boys and one girl."

We stared at each other in disbelief as we rocked in the cool winter air. I didn't know what was next for us, but at least we seemed to be aiming in the same direction.

"Should we go see what our parents are up to before someone comes to check on us again?" he asked.

"I mean, probably so," I replied. "But I'm enjoying this."

"Me too, Dr. Chris, but-"

"No need to say anything else, Charlie. Just promise me we can get a glider for whatever house we build."

"You want a big metal one or a wooden one?" he asked.

"Yes, please," I replied with a chuckle. Charlie, helped me up off the glider and held my hand as we exited the balcony and headed back downstairs to join his parents and probably mine.

———

They continued chatting with each other for another 30 minutes or so, only ending the conversation when my parents needed to travel to the extended family Christmas dinner. Charlie's family all took quick naps while I got the chance to help Grandma Elizabeth prepare Christmas dinner for their household, and by prepare, I mean I helped to keep her company as she cooked. She still wouldn't let me touch a thing. If she was anything like my grandmothers that was how she showed how much she cared. Her stories, much like theirs were a treat to listen to. They were reflective of a time now passed, but certainly offered a window into her soul and the heart of who she was.

Dinnertime arrived and we gathered once more to eat and fellowship. Charlie's parents wouldn't share much about their conversations with my parents, but they did share how much they were hoping to meet them in person some day. My second family was such a pleasure to get to know and I was so glad I said yes to Charlie's invitation to join him for Christmas. I knew that it would be hard to leave once the time came, but this trip could only be but so long. After dinner they all gathered around the television to watch one final Christmas movie together before we discussed the wake-up time for tomorrow morning and turning in for the night.

Christmas evening, Charlie and I showered, separately of course, so we wouldn't have to wake up extra early on the 26th. It's a good thing too because the two of us sat on top of the comforter and quilt, and chatted for hours about the events of the past 24 hours, about our families, and what was going to happen when we got back to Kansas City. He wanted to fix dinner for us at his place when my schedule allowed. I wanted to arrange a time for him to meet my family. We needed to celebrate Marlo's new position in Colorado before he left. Plus, there was still the matter of New Year's Eve, that we needed to figure out. Lots of details to iron out, but we were walking together in the same direction. Knowing that we needed to rise and drive in a few short hours, he and I finally decided to rest our heads for the night. We had been fighting sleep for a while, but we knew, or at least I did, that once our eyes closed for the night, this safe space where we'd been poured into and loved on by our families would soon be replaced by the stress of the real world.

We rose the next day to a 5:45 wake up call from his dad, who was an earlier riser just like his son. His mom and grandparents were already up as well and were waiting for us when we got downstairs with our bags. My feet felt heavy as we prepared to leave. I hadn't expected to find and love Charlie, and I sure hadn't counted on meeting his family so soon. So you know it wasn't in my plans yet to love them enough to tear up as we said goodbye for now. But it happened nonetheless.

I thanked them all for welcoming me into their home. Grandpa Charles hugged me first and I heard a quiver in his voice as he joked about me not letting Charlie fall asleep on the road. Next in the receiving line was Grandma Elizabeth, who hugged me like I was her own grandchild. It was almost like she knew that I hadn't had a grandmother's hug in years. She held me close in her arms and rocked me tenderly as she patted my back and told me that she loved me. Then there was Charlie's Dad, who'd shared a million jokes and laughs the entire visit. When it came time for me to say goodbye to him, he didn't have any words remaining, just one gigantic Dad hug. Finally, I stopped in front of Charlie's mom, who was wearing the pendant I had given her for Christmas.

She looked me in the eyes and thanked me for sharing time with them before holding on to me like she was truly going to miss my presence in the house. She discreetly whispered a brief message in my ear and tears welled up in my eyes. I nodded so she understood that I'd heard her loud and clear, then hugged her with all the heart that was left in me to spare. And with that, Charlie and I hit the road on the way back to Kansas City.

The two of us were quiet for the first 5 minutes of the trip on the way back to Highway 49, before Charlie decided to ask what his mom had said to me. "She told me that it was okay for me to not tell you what she said," I said, still wiping tears from my eyes. Charlie nodded and smiled, gingerly asking if I was okay.

"I am."

As we got on the highway, Charlie asked me to open the bag that was sitting between us. In it was a small breakfast feast, prepared by his mom and grandmother for our road trip back to Kansas City. I served him his breakfast burrito, which he ate as he drove. The potato rounds were perfectly fried and plentiful and the fruit smoothies they packed for us included energy boosting ingredients. Thankfully for the two of us, that worked for Charlie, but I was still sleepy from staying up the night before.

I had tried my hardest to stay awake to fulfill my promise to Grandpa Charles. Chief was such a smooth ride though. As Charlie drove, I drifted off to sleep, waking myself up after my head nodded so far down that my body instinctively jerked back upright.

Apparently it must have been a sight to see. Charlie got in a hearty chuckle at my expense but his empathy shined through as it had in every instance I could think of.

"You still have to work today. Why don't you go ahead and get some rest. I'll make sure we get back to Kansas City safely. There's a button on the side there that will recline your seat a bit if it helps." I nodded; exhausted, full and grateful to have such a caring partner by my side. I reclined the seat slightly and leaned my head back on the headrest, allowing the weight of my body to be cradled by the heated leather seats in his truck.

———

Can you imagine it? You're still getting to know someone after 3 days together and you voluntarily throw yourself into meeting and staying with their family over a major holiday. There is no rational explanation for that. The only thing that could make that possible is the force of nature that outlasts all humankind; the one thing you can invite into your life but can't dictate how swiftly it takes hold or stays. That unpredictable and incontestable force is love. There it was, carting me from one home to another and demonstrating its beauty and potential. My internal dialogue stopped trying to fight its validity and instead surrendered to all that could be.

CHAPTER 4
NEW YEAR'S EVE

It had been nearly a week since I dropped Dr. Chris off at her condo after our quick trip to spend Christmas with my family in Arkansas. She slept nearly the entire trip back to Kansas City, which gave me plenty of time to reflect.

I'm not sure what encouraged her to say yes, but I was glad that she did. It was my intention to show her just how much I appreciated her willingness to trust me enough to join me on a whim. I was nervous on the drive down, but my family welcomed her with open arms and her family seemed to get along well with mine, at least via video chat. She was a trooper for jumping in and I was honored to have the chance to share my family with her.

In the 5 days since we'd been back in Kansas City, the two of us had seen or spoken with each other every day. She was the first person I spoke with in the mornings and the last person I spoke with at night. I invited her over for dinner as promised, and got to show her the heirloom honeysuckle plant that had been passed down to me from my mom's family. The two story Tudor house that I bought when I moved to Kansas City felt more like home than it had in the entire two years I lived in it before meeting, Dr. Chris. I had tried my hardest to breathe life into the place. The lawn was thick and plush in the warmer months. The landscaping near the house was well kempt. The back patio held a fire pit area and bistro table. Inside, there was furniture and an assortment of houseplants that I had managed to actually keep alive. There was life in this house, but something had always been missing.

The moment she stepped foot inside these walls after a long day at the hospital, I was hit with a moment of clarity. I knew exactly what had been missing. I had all this space and nobody to share it with. I'd had Oakley visit me before, but the feeling wasn't the same. Dr. Chris' presence was the missing element. She was the proverbial love that was missing. When I welcomed her in, it felt like she had come home, to me.

"Your house is amazing, Charlie!" she told me, with excitement in her eyes. "So where's the dino-line?" she joked. I took her on a tour of the place, taking great care to show her where the bat-phone was located. She complimented something in every space she saw, including the office that held my old school phone tapped into the landline. I didn't understand how one person could have such a tremendous impact on my life, especially in just two weeks. She had rolled into my life like the snowstorm that trapped us at her condo and now I couldn't imagine what things would look like without her around.

The next four days flew by. We dined and laughed on the 27th, and made plans to do the same over lunch with Marlo on the 28th. We were stood up by Marlo, but lunch at the Fresh Pantry was good. It was a bit surreal to return to the site of our first date, but I enjoyed the flashback and new memories we were making together. Just as they did on our first date, her eyes held a glimmer of light in them when she laughed. I spent nearly the entire lunch trying to see how long I could get them to shine.

We ended up helping Marlo pack up the rest of his place on the 29th and ate some take out as we worked. Watching the two of them joke together gave me some insight as to what Dr. Chris was like as a child. They had inside jokes for days and I appreciated what he added to her life. After hearing some of their stories, I was grateful they had each other growing up.

On the 30th, Dr. Chris and I only had the chance to chat on the phone, but it gave me time to prepare for what she and I had planned for the last day of the year. Her mom and sister invited us to ring in the New Year with their families, which meant I needed to use the 30th to wrap up my end of year house maintenance. When I bought this place, my dad and grandfather gave me a checklist and schedule to adhere to, so I could keep the house in good working order and tip top shape. The end of year maintenance was a way to start the year fresh.

Check the gutters for leaves and ice dams. Check for drafts around doors and windows - caulk where needed. Cover the AC unit. Swap out the HVAC filter. Look for leaks in little used toilets and sinks. Test the smoke and carbon-monoxide detectors. Double check the hose bibs outside to ensure they're still covered. Clean the dryer exhaust. I did all of that in addition to ensuring that the house itself was clean, which made for a long hard day.

Dr. Chris offered to come help, and as much as I wanted to see her, I knew that I'd have a different set of priorities if she were present. I'm not saying she was a distraction, but I knew that my focus would be skewed. Knowing that we hadn't had another official date since picking out Randolph, our Christmas Tree, I promised her that New Year's Day would be our day. But meeting her family came first.

I picked her up in the truck and she guided me through the city to her parent's house. I checked out the landscaping surrounding their split level home. All of the shrubs and trees were well established and perfectly manicured. Someone was making a statement about who lived there.

Dr. Chris sat still in the car before turning towards me and speaking, "I don't think they've seen us yet, we can always back out of the driveway and come back in a few minutes." She seemed unusually nervous about the prospect of me meeting her parents.

"You okay, Sugarplum?" I asked her.

"Yeah, I'm fine. I just know -" she paused. I looked for the answer in her eyes.

"I'm right here, Chris. What is it?"

One deep breath helped her summon the courage to share what was on her mind. "I just know they're going to see in you what your parents saw in me."

I grinned through my words. "So you're saying they're going to love me?" I asked, pulling a chuckle from Dr. Chris.

"They're absolutely going to love you. Then there's the whole, starting the new year with you, thing."

I was intrigued, "What thing?"

Her face contorted, "How do you feel about kissing me in front of my family?"

"Oh, that thing. Let's just feel it out. No pressure." I said as Dr. Chris nodded, still looking full of nerves. I held her hand and asked if she was ready.

A shallow exhale let me know just how anxious she was. "They just peeked out of the house."

I hopped out of the truck and walked to her side, opening the door and offering her my hand as usual. Dr. Chris seized my hand before hopping out and squeezing it all the way to the front door. I weaved our fingers together to let her know that I was with her, every step of the way.

The front door swung open before we could ring the doorbell. Dr. Chris' mom stepped out and hugged her daughter tightly, "Hi, baby girl!"

"Hi, Mom!!" she said hugging her mom with one arm while still clutching my hand. I tried to shake it free, so she could hug her with both arms, but it was clear to me that Dr. Chris was not interested in letting go.

"Hey Charlie! It's so good to meet you in person," she said before hugging me with the same zeal in which she hugged her daughter. "You two come inside. Come out of the cold."

"Thank you," I said as calmly as possible. I had inadvertently absorbed some of Dr. Chris' nervous energy and was doing my best to push through it.

Dr. Chris took my coat, scarf, and gloves, placing them on a hanger in the coat closet. I helped her with her coat and her Dad joined us in their entryway from around the corner.

"There they are," he said greeting his daughter with a hug before turning and extending a hand towards me. "ChARlie, so nice to meet you," he said while firmly shaking my hand.

"It's nice to meet you too, sir," I said, returning the clasp.

"Well, come on in here. We were just

watching the news." He shuffled past their formal living room and had a seat in his recliner in the family room.

"I thought you were going to take them downstairs to the basement, Walter."

"Oh, I figured Chris could help you with a few things in the kitchen before we headed down there." That was man code for have a seat son, I want to talk to you about your intentions with my daughter.

"Be kind to Charlie," her mom said. She ushered me to a seat on the couch before leaving the room.

Dr. Chris, ducked into the kitchen with her mom and the two of them were clinking around, setting things up for tonight. I made the mistake of watching her walk away. Not a good start to the conversation with her dad.

"You like what you see, Charlie?"

"Sorry, sir," I said, embarrassed to have been caught gazing at my love in front of her father. Suddenly the idea of kissing her at midnight caused me a little anxiety as well.

"You know, Charlie, my daughter has only brought one other person to the house like this. He had us all fooled." *I see we're getting straight to business.*

"She told me about what happened with Trevor," I said as irritation filled my body.

"She did?" he asked, surprised that I knew his name. I nodded before he continued, "I think he hurt us just as much as he hurt Chris. I told him he could call me Dad, the first time I met him. So pardon me if I don't extend that same courtesy to you."

"I understand, sir."

"I treated him like family, Charlie and he treated her like she was disposable."

"He makes it really hard on those of us who are in it for the right reasons."

Mr. James nodded his head. "One thing I never had the chance to do with the last guy," he refused to call him by name, "was meet his parents." I wasn't 100% sure where he was going, but I had an idea. "I appreciated the chance to chat with your parents last week."

"My dad said the same thing about the two of you last week."

He continued, "I have a better idea of who you are after chatting with them. We had a good conversation about what it was like to date back in the day. I can't imagine what it's like to date nowadays."

"It's definitely not for the faint of heart. That's for sure. I'm hoping I don't have to worry about too much more of that, though." *Why did I say that?*

He sat up in his chair and leaned in my direction. "Is that right?"

I took a deep swallow and cleared my throat, "Yes, sir." He studied my face and nodded, not saying a word. All of the sudden my lungs felt like they weren't working correctly.

He extended a bit of grace and changed the subject. "Charlie, your mom told me that you left your job in Corporate America in favor of becoming an educator."

"Yes sir, I did," I said, my breathing returning to normal.

"Mmm hmmm," he looked like he wanted more information, but was hesitant to ask.

I offered the info myself, "I was making good money and was great at my job, but I just didn't feel like I was making an impact on the world."

"Is that right?"

"Yes sir. I just felt like I was helping money circulate, not that it's a bad thing, but it wasn't the type of footprint that I was hoping to leave behind. I had a summer experience where I got to help encourage the love of reading in elementary aged kids. It changed my life. In college I didn't see myself as an educator, but I guess He had other plans for me."

"That's admirable, Charlie. Now, educators don't get paid their worth. Are you doing okay?"

"Oh, yes sir. When I was working in Corporate America, I was pretty aggressive on both my retirement and multiple savings accounts, so I was able to buy my house outright when I moved to Kansas City."

"A man who knows what he values, huh?" I was nervous to do so, but I smiled anyway.

"Yes sir. That's something my parents encouraged me to figure out pretty early. You can pivot around a solid core, but if you don't know what your core is, you just drift all over the place. I'm not interested in drifting. I'm ready to put down roots."

"We taught Chris to do the same thing," he said before pausing and leaning back in his chair. "I can see why my daughter is drawn to you." I waited anxiously to hear what else was on his mind. His eyebrows scrunched like he was trying to decide how much to say to me. "She's my baby girl, Charlie."

"I understand, sir." At least I thought I did. Nothing, no amount of foresight could have prepared me for the information he shared next.

"She's the one that taught us the most

about ourselves and life." I nodded, as I listened to him tell me about the time they thought they'd lost her, "She was a climber, from the time she was born. She climbed up on everything she could find. I can't tell you the number of times I caught her from a fall. But one day I wasn't there." He began to get choked up as he recalled the event like it happened yesterday. "She was 5 years old and she and Yvonne were playing out in the backyard. I was getting ready to cut the grass, so I was gassing up the lawn mower. Her mom was inside on the phone with her mother. Nothing abnormal, you know. But Chris, she climbed that tree back there and just got too high up for her own good."

"Oh no."

"She hasn't told you this story?" he asked, his eyebrows raised towards the sky.

"No sir."

"Well, maybe I should save it for her to tell you."

"I," my brain was moving a mile a minute and I was having trouble formulating a complete thought, "did she fall?"

"She did," he continued. "She fell from that branch that's missing its leaves," he said pointing to the tree in the backyard. That branch must have been a solid 12 feet off the ground.

"How did she climb that high?"

"Lord knows, Charlie. She climbed it so fast too. All I heard was her body hitting the ground and I took off running around to the back of the house. When I got back there she wasn't breathing."

Hearing it knocked the wind from my lungs. "Oh my God."

"Her mother saw her as she fell and hung up the phone, but she couldn't get out to her fast enough to break her fall. I was afraid to move her and afraid not to." Tears started welling in my eyes as his voice broke. "One of our neighbors called 911 for us and the paramedics came in about 3 minutes. The longest 3 minutes of my life. She didn't breathe the entire time. Lucille took Vonnie inside so she wouldn't see anything. They pumped oxygen into her lungs to see if they could get her to breathe and brought a stretcher around to stabilize her little body before taking her around to the ambulance. I rode with Chris, and 'Cille & Vonnie rode behind us. She was so still in the ambulance, Charlie. I thought she was gone."

I looked back at Dr. Chris as she stood in the kitchen and turned back to her dad who continued his story. "She looked like she was gone. They got her to the hospital in no time and took her back to figure out what was going on. She was in there for almost an hour. That was almost an hour with no word and me thinking the worst. The doctor came out and asked if we were her parents and they told me that they were able to get her to breathe. Said she had fractured a few vertebrae in her spine and had suffered a serious head injury. He told us that she wouldn't be the same child we knew before the accident and that we would need to take it one day at a time."

"Dr. Chris had told me that she got into an accident when she was younger and that the nurses and doctors took such good care of her that she wanted to do that for other kids. She didn't tell me how bad it was."

"When you have kids, you already learn to slow down. This though, this gave us a greater appreciation of life. Her rehab was long, but eventually she was walking and running and tumbling like every other kid her age. I'm not sure what she experienced when she wasn't breathing. She never told us about what that was like. She drew some pictures a few times, but she wouldn't talk about them. I asked her what she remembered about it and she would just shrug. Whatever it was though gave her laser focus. She flew through college and med school. She didn't fear much of anything, probably because she had already stared death in the face." I nodded in stunned silence.

"That's why we love her so fiercely, Charlie."

"I had no idea," I said again turning my head in her direction. I was in love with a walking miracle.

"Uh oh," her dad chuckled. "She's already got you hasn't she?" I turned my head sharply in his direction, feeling like a kid who got caught with his hand in the cookie jar. All I could do was smile sheepishly.

"I've never had a connection like this

with anyone before." He nodded.

"That's how I felt about her mother when I met her. I wasn't against children before, but I never saw myself as anything more than someone's uncle. Then all of the sudden I was dreaming about taking our future children home to visit their grandparents. Her Daddy told me that he could see it on my face. Now I get it. I see it."

All I could do was laugh and rub the back of my head. He saw himself in me. That could work in my favor or against it depending on what portion of that he focused on.

"She's precious Charlie."

"Yes, sir. I mean, I thought she was before, now I understand just how precious she is."

He nodded. "So, Charlie, should we move this party to the basement before Vonnie and her family get here?"

"I'm ready when you are. Should we see if there's anything we can take downstairs?"

"That's a good idea." The two of us found our way into the kitchen. Her dad greeted his wife with a kiss on the cheek.

"Did you two have a good chat?" she asked, looking in my direction.

"It was a good chat," her dad replied.

"I was talking to Charlie, Walter."

"It was a good chat," I reiterated as Dr. Chris' father nodded in solidarity. Dr. Chris, looked for confirmation that I was okay and I found myself caught in a gaze of admiration.

"Can we grab anything from you and take it downstairs?" he asked them. They loaded us up with food that they had been busy chopping and arranging, and we took it downstairs to the finished basement, spreading out the food across the bar.

Her sister Vonne and her family found their way downstairs when they arrived and I had the chance to meet her and the twins, Christina, named after her aunt, and Corwin, named after his great grandfather. They were full of energy and excited that they got to stay up until midnight, but more excited to hang out with their Aunt Chris.

The two of them warmed up to me pretty quickly and eventually we found ourselves in a rousing game of Charades. We laughed and snacked, and laughed some more, then Vonne pulled me aside to chat.

"So Dad told me that you're really into my sister." I was caught off guard. She didn't beat around the bush.

"I am," I said definitively, hoping that was enough to demonstrate my love, but knowing that if someone was bold enough to cut straight to the chase like that, there were probably more questions to come.

"Does she know it, Charlie?"

"I told her on Christmas Eve, and have tried my hardest to show her every day since."

"If you hurt her heart, I know people," she was straight faced. "You feel me?"

"I don't have any plans to hurt her, Vonne."

"Easier said than done, Charlie," she said with hurt in her voice.

"I feel you, Vonne," I replied, not knowing what damage had been done to her, or if her comments were a reflection of the damage that Trevor had done to their family. What a crappy wake for them to be caught in. It's a good thing my intentions were pure. I wished I could just wipe his actions from their memories, but I certainly understood why they were all so protective of Dr. Chris.

———

She and I hadn't had much time to ourselves that evening. I bounced between entertaining the twins, and holding conversations with her parents and sister and I honestly can't say that I minded it. They all shared stories about Chris that helped me get to know her a little bit better. It was that conversation with her dad that stuck with me the most. I wanted to ask her about it, but I figured she would tell me when she felt comfortable doing so.

As it always seemed to do when we were together, time moved swiftly. Before we knew it there were only 15 minutes remaining in the year. She and I still hadn't had time to ourselves yet, so I made eyes with her from across the basement. She excused herself from the game of Go Fish with her niece and nephew, and delivered a paper plate full of popcorn to my lap.

"How you doin', Charlie?" she asked.

"I'm okay," I replied, slightly exhausted by the day.

She patted my leg. "Just okay?" she asked with a hint of worry.

"Yes, I-" I hesitated. She lowered her head and looked in my eyes. I finished my original thought, "I'm okay."

"It's a lot, I know. They're a lot," she said, speaking of her family.

"With good reason," I said, completely understanding where they were coming from. "It's fine."

She shook her head in dissent, "I should've spent more time with you tonight."

I understood where she was coming from, but I wanted her to know that I wasn't concerned in the least. "No. You haven't spent time with them in a while. You spent time exactly where it was needed."

"Charlie, we can spend time with them together," she offered.

"We can now, Chris. But they needed time with you separately, to check in with you and know that you're happy. And they needed separate time with me to ensure that my heart is in it, that I'm in it for the right reasons." She nodded and reached out for my hand.

"They all told me that they really like you, Charlie," she said with her hypnotic stare.

"That's a relief," I laughed, hoping to break free from her trance.

"I enjoyed watching you with my family tonight."

"I enjoyed spending time with them, with you." We spent a bit of time sharing more about the conversations we each had with her family members while snacking on the popcorn she'd brought to me. "Did you make this popcorn?" I asked her.

A look of concern filled her face, "Why?"

"It tastes like the popcorn from our Marathon Movie Night."

"I didn't make this popcorn," she paused, a childlike smile filled her face. "Mom made this batch, but thank you. She makes the best popcorn so I'll take that as a compliment."

Time passed on and before I knew it we were down to 5 minutes left in the year.

"So, my family has a tradition of closing out the year by celebrating the greatest thing about this year," I told her.

"Yeah?"

"Mmm hmm. What was the greatest thing about this year for you, Dr. Chris?"

She paused, pretending that she was deep in thought, "Maybe Marley?"

"Marley was pretty triumphant. That's a good one," I said, still munching away on the popcorn.

She pinched me on my arm.

"What?"

"What was the greatest thing about this year for you, Charlie?"

I couldn't contain my smile. It was semi-permanent. Before I could respond, Corwin found his way to my lap. "Uncle Charlie!" That caught me off guard. I looked at Dr. Chris, who had stars in her eyes. "There's only 1 minute left before New Years! Come on, we need some toast!"

"Okay, Corwin, let's go get some toast. Dr. Chris, come with us. You need some toast too!"

We found our way to the bar to grab our glasses for the toast, and the countdown began. I glanced around the room at her family. Her mom and dad snuggled up to each other behind the bar. Her sister and the twins snuggled up together with their glasses in hand. They made it to 20 seconds and counting while I tried to gauge how Dr. Chris was feeling, recalling that she was nervous about a New Year's kiss.

There we stood in the middle of her family. I held her hand in mine and gazed into her eyes. "Dr. Chris."

They were filled with so much hope as she returned my stare, "Charlie."

The twins shouted, "10-9-8"

"It was you," I told her.

"6-"

"What was me?"

"4-3"
I rushed to beat the clock. "The best part of my year was you."

"HAPPY NEW YEAR!!!!"

She wrapped an arm around my neck and kissed me with unrelenting passion. I suddenly forgot that we were sharing space with her family and I returned the intensity.

"You used to kiss me like that, Walter!" her mom teased.

"I'll kiss you like that tonight once all these children are gone," he said as they laughed together.

I pulled back. "It seems we have an audience ma'am," I said giving her one final peck. Her niece and nephew giggled.

"Uncle Charlie, we need the toast!" We clinked glasses and her father toasted to a year full of good health, wellness, and memories that will last a lifetime.

I had something in mind that I hoped would take care of the latter.

Chapter 5

New Year's Day

Dr. Chris:

Charlie was the best New Year's Eve date. We spent the evening with my family. I know it doesn't seem like the most romantic ordeal, but watching how patient he was as they questioned him to the nth degree, and seeing him love on my niece and nephew was good for my heart. I found myself whispering stethoscope several times throughout the night.

When the two of us finally created space for each other, Charlie told me that he was okay, but he looked tired. I'd hoped that

I hadn't rushed this meeting. I'd hoped that it hadn't overwhelmed him. But he assured me that he was okay. And when Corwin called him Uncle Charlie and jumped on his lap, I saw his face dance again. First a little bit of shock, then a bit of caution, and finally it rested upon joy. When I saw how Corwin's joy also brought joy to him, I knew that the feeling of home I had experienced prior to meeting his parents was real. I was falling deeper and deeper, and I couldn't see the bottom. That thought was slightly terrifying, but I had made a promise to do whatever was in my power to make it work.

Vonne had pulled me to the side earlier that night and asked me how I felt about him.

"I could see it on your face on Christmas Day," she said. "But seeing you in person is a whole other level, Chris. What do you want to happen here?"

I wasn't sure how to answer her question. "What are you asking me, Vonne?"

"I'm asking, where do you see this going?"

I didn't answer her. I couldn't answer her. Charlie and I hadn't formally discussed the long term. We'd spoken in code about it on the phone before Christmas, but I wouldn't call that a formal discussion by any stretch of the word.

"I see a long term relationship with Charlie."

"Long term dating or long term like Mom and Dad?" she asked through furrowed eyebrows.

"Mom and Dad."

I don't think she was expecting that to be my answer. "Oh, does he know?"

"Yeah, he knows."

"Does he feel the same way? Do you know that yet? Guys can be kind of cryptic when they're uncomfortable."

"Yeah."

"Wait. Yeah he feels the same way or yeah they're cryptic?"

"Yeah he feels the same way, Vonne," I said, slightly annoyed to be having this conversation with my sister. It almost felt like she didn't fully trust my judgment.

"Chris! Why haven't I met him before today?"

"Because I didn't meet him until mid-December."

Her jaw hit the floor and I stared at her blank faced. "Are you telling me that you just met this man and already he's taken you home to meet his parents?"

"Yes, and they've never met anyone he's dated before. Even his high school girlfriends."

"So, wait."

"Vonne!"

"No, Chris. You remember, Trevor."

"I do remember, Trevor. He and I were going through the motions."

"So you're telling me that you didn't

love him?"

"I'm telling you that I did love him, but it was a different type of love than Charlie."

"How can you even know you love him? You literally just met him!"

"Did Jason know that he loved Christina and Corwin the first day he met them?" I asked referencing her husband, who was currently stationed overseas. "You told me he didn't know about the twins until after they were born because you didn't want him to worry about you while there was nothing he could do about it."

"I did. He was in Kabul, where all the action was. I needed him to focus on coming back home alive."

"And he did. He focused on coming home to you. But when he got home, he met his son and daughter for the first time. And did he love them instantly?"

"He did."

"So what's the difference?" I asked defiantly.

"This was his family."

"And Charlie is mine."

"We're your family, Chris."

"Charlie is home, Vonne. Don't ask me how I know. I just do."

I think she finally got it. But she, like everyone else was cautious after Trevor had duped them, all of us really, into thinking he was a worthy man during the time we shared together.

"I've never heard you call someone home before, Chris," she said. I shrugged.

"I've never felt like anyone was home except y'all. But look at him over there, laughing with Mom and Dad. You saw him with your kids."

"I did," she said confidently.

"Tell me I'm wrong."
"I can't." She hugged me and told me to let her know what I needed and I promised to do just that.

Mom and I had a similar conversation before Vonne and the kids arrived. Dad had signaled that he wanted to chat with Charlie in private and I went to help mom in the kitchen. The two of us were chopping veggies and popping popcorn when she asked me point blank if I loved him. You know as well as I do that if your momma's asking you if you love someone, she likely already knows that you do. So what's the point in trying to dance around the question? I answered just as bluntly as she'd asked me, "I do."

"Have you made room for him?" I looked at her, my eyes full of question. She added more context to help explain her thoughts, "You choose what's high priority and what isn't. Does he know where he falls on the spectrum of your priorities? Have you made him 2nd, 3rd, 4th?"

I nodded. Understanding what she was nudging me towards. I guess I had made him 2nd priority over the last week, but before Christmas he went from top billing to the understudy.

Dad and I had the chance to chat briefly, but he was a man of few words when it came to me and the choices I made in my life. He only encouraged me to follow my gut when it came to Charlie and I knew what he was saying. I hadn't listened to my gut with Trevor and that was a train wreck that could have been avoided, had I not tried to intercede with "logic."

The common thread through all of their conversations was twofold. First, their assessment of how I really felt about Charlie, and second they shared just how much they cared about him after having had the chance to chat with him and watch how he interacted with everyone else. So when I finally had the chance to serve him some popcorn and chat, I was able to reassure him that they liked him. When he asked me about my favorite part of this year, my gut knew it was him but instead I answered, Marley. A broad smile painted his face when I asked the same question of him. He was just about to answer when Corwin hopped in his lap, both saving and making his day.

I had hoped he would be able to keep his family's tradition alive during this celebration, but the countdown had begun and he still hadn't answered the question. I had planned to ask him on New Year's Day if he didn't get the chance to share it. That way we could still somewhat keep the tradition alive. But with seven seconds to go in the year, he blurted out, "It was you." I wasn't sure I knew what he was talking about, so I asked for clarification.

"What was me?"

With two seconds to go and just one statement, he filled my heart with passion that came spilling over the sides. "The best part of my year was you." I needed to hear it, and didn't even know.

After everyone raised their glasses and toasted to the new year, I whispered to Charlie, "Me too," and watched a contented and lopsided smile appear on the right side of his face. He was full.

"I love you, Chris." Those were the first words he spoke to me in the New Year, just before his phone rang. It was his mom calling to wish him a Happy New Year. They spoke on the phone for a spell before he passed it to me. "She asked to speak with you."

"Hello? Happy New Year, Mrs. Hughes! Yes, mom. We're at my parents' house celebrating with my family. Sure, hold on just a second and I'll pass the phone to them," I said looking at Charlie with wonder. I handed the phone to my parents and slid into the background as they all wished each other a Happy New Year. Mom called me back to get Charlie's phone, letting me know in the process that his mom asked to speak with me again, which left Charlie looking a little confused.

"You remember what I told you, Chris," she said to me.

"Yes ma'am. I will," I promised her.

"Hug and kiss my son for me and tell him we'll speak again soon."

"Oh he's right here. Let me hand him, - okay. Okay, I will. Love you too," I replied before handing Charlie his phone back.

"She didn't even say goodbye to her only son?"

Giggling, I delivered the message she'd sent to him via me, "She said she'll speak with you again soon."

He kissed me on the temple and shook his head. "I've always been the favorite child. I don't know if I can take being second favorite in the eyes of the woman who gave birth to me," he joked.

We hung out with my family for another hour before heading out into the world. We hadn't discussed whether or not we'd return to my condo or his house, but the two of us hopped in his truck and just drove for a bit. Our impromptu tour took us past the lights on The Plaza, through downtown, and eventually we found our way to a bridge that allowed us to overlook the city and all of the people who were headed back to their homes following a night of celebration. There was much for us to celebrate, but we just stood still taking in the world for a moment. Around 2 in the morning I yawned and Charlie asked me if I was ready to go home. I nodded and told him I needed the closest bed. That happened to be his and I knew it. He drove us to his house and helped me out of his truck holding me up as we walked through the front door together.

I hadn't seen his bedroom before today,

but I had a feeling that was all about to change. "Charlie, I can sleep on the couch."

"Nonsense, Chris. I'll sleep on the couch. You need to rest."

"I'm fine sleeping on the couch, really. This is your house. You should sleep in your own bed."

"My house. My rules," he said through nervous laughter.

It should be noted that when I'm sleepy, I become far more silly than my normal waking self.

"Yes, father," I said to him in reply.

"Oh, don't start that mess, ma'am. Your sleepy butt needs to lay down."

He walked me upstairs to the master bedroom and opened the door, refusing to enter in there with me. His feet still in the hallway, he leaned inside and pointed out the doorway to the bathroom. "...that way you won't have to search down the hallway for a bathroom in the middle of the night."

I nodded. "Charlie, I don't have any pajamas."

His eyes brightened, "Sure you do. Second drawer of my dresser is full of t-shirts. Feel free to grab one of those. Last drawer is full of basketball shorts with drawstrings because we are nowhere near the same size. You have your pick."

The thought of falling asleep in clothes that smelled like Charlie was comforting.

"I'll be in the room across the hallway with the door open. Just holler if you need anything, okay?" I nodded.

"Okay, Charlie."

"Hey Sugarplum, do me a favor?"

"What's that, Charlie?"

"Hand me those clothes on the end of the bed. Those are MY pj's." I retrieved and handed them to Charlie from just inside the threshold of the door.

"Thank you. Sleep well, beautiful."

"I will, Charlie," I paused, gazing up into his eyes. "Thank you."

"For what?" he asked, giving my face a once over.

"Goodnight," I said after giving him a quick peck on the cheek.

I got ready for bed and crawled under the freshly cleaned comforter and sheets, and before my head could hit the pillow, I was sound asleep.

I hoped I would wake up before him, but I smelled bacon cooking as the sunlight from his window kissed my eyelids. I lay still in his room, taking in as much detail as I could. I had missed it last night, but he had a picture of us by the bed. It was the one of us gazing into each other's eyes in front of the massive Christmas Tree in Union Station. I was staring at the photo when I heard his feet walking up the creaky wooden staircase. I closed my eyes and pretended to be sleep when he knocked on the door.

I heard it crack just a little and Charlie, quietly call for me, "Dr. Chris." I stayed as still as I could. "Dr. Chris, I'm going to open the door." I lay as relaxed as possible and listened as Charlie spoke his thoughts out loud, "My God, you're so beautiful." There was a gap of time between that statement and the next. I can only imagine he must have been gazing upon me. "How do I wake you up without coming in the room? Do I drop something? That might startle her." I turned on my side. "Dr. Chris?" he asked with a knock on the bedroom door.

———

Charlie:

I started the year with her. Ella Fitzgerald's song that followed us around on our first and second dates had me eagerly anticipating the day. I wasn't sure what New Year's Eve would hold, but we'd heard the song so much that I knew we were supposed to spend it together. Much like every other date we'd experienced in this relationship, people poured into us, and both Dr. Chris and I were emotionally full by the end of the night. I hadn't planned on kissing her at midnight unless she was open to it. We were at her parents' house and in front of all her family, which I thought might be uncomfortable. But I was thunderstruck when she reached out for me. I didn't want to leave her hanging, so I poured out my emotions into her in the presence of God and all her kin.

My mom called after midnight this year. She told me she didn't want to interrupt our midnight kiss and I wasn't sure how to respond. By the time they passed the phone around to spread New Year wishes, I knew what I wanted to say. But mom sent a message to me through Dr. Chris, told her that she loved her and got off the phone, ignoring her only child. This was the first time she'd asked specifically to chat with someone I was in a relationship with. Dr. Chris, my heart, was valued by my family just as much as she was valued by me. Yep. This was completely different.

When we left that evening, I shook hands with her dad and thanked him for our chat. "Of course, son," he replied, bringing me in for a hug. I knew that was major for him and I didn't take it lightly at all.

I helped Dr. Chris in the truck and we took off on a tour of Kansas City, stopping on a bridge that was over the highway. We watched the traffic pass by and I wondered silently where everyone was going and what their story was. She yawned and I knew it was time for us to choose our next adventure. She asked for the closest bed, which we both knew was mine. So I drove the two of us to my house, internally struggling to figure out the sleeping arrangement. She told me that she was cool with the couch, but that wasn't an option for me. I could put her in one of the guest rooms, but she was sleepier then I'd ever seen her and I wasn't sure she'd know where to find the bathroom if she needed it. That left the option that would be most comfortable for her, my room. I showed her where to find something to sleep in and told her where she could find me if she needed me.

I tried to go to sleep that night. I really did. But I kept an ear open so that I could be alert enough to respond in case she needed something. It was probably 2:30 or so when I laid down for bed. But around 6:30, when it was clear to me that I was only going to sleep in 20 minute spurts, I crawled out of the guest bed and crept down my creaky stairs to the living room.

Around 7:00 I got hungry and started fixing us some breakfast. By 7:30 it was nearly ready so I snuck back upstairs in hopes of waking, Dr. Chris. She didn't respond when I called her name or when I knocked on the door. So I cracked it open and attempted to wake her with both again. Nothing. I fully opened the door and there she was, the sunlight caressing her face just as it had when she was sleeping in my arms in her condo the day we got snowed in. She was just as beautiful this morning as she was on that afternoon. I don't know if I said it out loud or if it stayed in my head, but I couldn't help but think it; my God was she beautiful. I just watched her sleep for a while and hoped she didn't catch me looking. She turned over and I called her name. She blinked her eyes open and smiled at me.

"Good morning, Charlie. What time is it?"

"Good morning, Dr. Chris. It's time for breakfast."

"Do you want some help fixing it?" she asked extending an arm in my direction.

I walked into the room and pulled her upright in the bed. She patted the mattress beside her for me to sit down. "I got us, remember."

She nodded and rubbed the same space she had just patted. I sat down and told her that I couldn't stay long because there was bacon that needed flipping. She slowly extended an arm and lightly rubbed my back. I knew I would be under her spell if I stayed. I needed to get up from the bed, but my legs weren't working. It was already happening. I turned to face her so I could tell her that I needed to check on the bacon, but the sight of her face held me in place. Nothing came out of my mouth. She leaned in and planted a sweet kiss on my lips.

"Alright now woman!" I said hopping up. "Meet me in the kitchen in 5 minutes?"

She nodded, "I'll see you there." I left the room as quickly as I could, hoping she hadn't read too far into my hasty exit.

Five minutes passed and I was downstairs in my kitchen setting the table and preparing some fresh juice when I heard her hustling down the stairs. I turned around to see her bopping into the room through a beam of sunlight, hair up, barefoot and wearing one of my old college t shirts and some shorts from about the same time period. Both were far too big for her, but were probably the smallest in size that were in my dresser. It was comfortable, like something we'd done hundreds of times before, but the truth is, this was a first.

"This kitchen smells fantastic!" she said as she found her way into the vintage booth in the corner. "Did you just fix this juice?" she asked as I set the glass on the table in front of her. I answered with a nod. "What did I do to deserve all of this?"

"Who said you need to have done something special to deserve to be treated like this regularly?"

"Well Happy New Year to me!" she chuckled, leaning in for another kiss. I didn't stop her. I felt a little more confident in my ability to keep it respectful when we weren't sitting on a bed. "Thank you, Charlie."

"Mmm hmmm. Of course! Would you like to say the blessing for us?"

She blessed the food and the two of us ate breakfast and laughed about the events of the last 24 hours. I got a reminder on my phone for Jax's 8th birthday party and asked if she wanted to join me. She was in, and we made a plan for me to get cleaned up here and for us to make our way back to the condo so she could get cleaned up.

I found her on the couch watching the Rose Parade after I was finished showering and getting dressed. I sat down and watched a bit with her. Asking how soon she wanted to leave. It was an unusually warm January day, which funny enough, wasn't unusual for Kansas City.

"What time do we need to get there?" she asked me. I was open. The party started at 2:00, but we could get there as early as she wanted.

"How long do you think it'll take to get there from the condo?"

"Probably about 15 minutes. Not too long at all."

"What if we try to get there around a quarter 'til?"

"So leave the condo at 1:30?"

"Yes."

"And how long do you need to get ready?"

She looked at me and laughed and I knew she was thinking about how she'd gotten ready for a date in 5 minutes. I shook my head at the thought of how quickly she had showered and dressed.

"Let me rephrase that. How much time do you want to get ready?"

"Let's say thirty minutes just to be safe."

"So we need to make sure you're back at the condo by 12:50 so you have some wiggle room."

"Sounds about right."

"Let's leave here at 12:30 then."

We lounged around until it was time to get moving, then drove across town to her condo, where I continued to lounge until it was time for us to go to Steve and Sabrina's house. I hadn't seen them since the day I saw Dr. Chris hugging Marlo in the hospital. It just occurred to me that they had absolutely no idea what had transpired in the last week. They only knew I was going home for Christmas.

I told Dr. Chris that we'd have some explaining to do when we got there and apologized for not giving them a heads up. She asked if it would be awkward for her to be there and I told her that I didn't think so. We were about to test that theory.

We pulled up in their driveway at a quarter til, and Jax's head popped up in the window. He turned back towards the interior of the house and shouted something before turning back around and waving in our direction. Sabrina came to the window and waved, then turned her head around to shout something to Steve before facing us again with a broad smile.

I hopped out of the truck to get the door for Dr. Chris, extending a hand to help her get out. She grabbed Jax's birthday present and we walked towards the front door, which swung open before we could ring the doorbell. That was twice in less than 24 hours.

Sabrina answered the door with a hug for each of us, "Hi, Dr. Chris! Hi, Charlie!"

"Happy New Year," Dr. Chris wished her as she returned the hug.

"Hey Sabrina, Happy New Year," I said as she looked at me like she needed to know what happened immediately.

"Dr. Chris, Jax and Steve are inside. I'm sure Jax will find you," she said as she closed the door behind us and pulled me into the living room where we had our last chat. "Charlie."

"Yes?" I replied waiting for the inevitable litany of questions that I knew were forthcoming.

"Don't give me that. The last we knew, you were headed home for Christmas."

"I went there."

"What happened? How did we end up here?" Sabrina asked with her arms raised in question.

I cracked a slight smile, knowing the

information I was about to tell her would sound ridiculous. "I heard your voice telling me to stay open and I prayed for a sign. As soon as I was done praying, I got a text from her with a link to a video montage of the two of us cutting down Randolph."

Her eyebrows did jumping jacks across her brow ridge. "Randolph?"

"The Christmas Tree. Different story. Stay focused, Sabrina," I laughed.

She looked at her watch, then back at me, with a slow blink, "I got time."

"So I had the chance to see what our date looked like from the outside in, instead of the inside out. I saw how she looked at me and I knew that I must have missed something when I saw her at the hospital. So I made a plan to call her on Christmas Eve, but she got the inside scoop from Marley on how I felt and she updated the list with a request for some cider."

"What list?" Sabrina asked.

"The list. The list. Stay with me," I emphasized with hands that looked like they were shaking an invisible box in front of me. Her face looked befuddled, but I continued nonetheless, "So I went to see her at the hospital and asked her to come with me to my parents' house that afternoon."

"In Arkansas?!" she asked.

"Yes."

Her voice seemed to rise an octave with each question. "And she said, yes?"

"Yes."

"On Christmas Eve?"

"Yes," I nodded.

"Had you asked her to go with you before you got to the hospital?"

"No. I hadn't even considered it until I saw her."

"Then you just blurted it out," she stated, her voice returning to its normal range. No question embedded in there at all.

"You know me so well," I smirked.

She twirled her hand in my direction. "I know. Continue."

"So we went to my parents' house that night and came back on the morning of the 26th."

"She didn't spend Christmas with her family?" she asked, her voice rising again.

"I mean, she spent it with her extended family."

Sabrina finally cracked a smile, "They loved her?"

"Like they gave birth to her," I affirmed with a nod and a wide grin.

"Oh Charlie, I'm so happy for you! Wait, have you met her family yet?"

"I met them last night."

She leaned back into the window seat, raising a single eyebrow in my direction, "No fancy soiree for New Year's Eve?"

"I much preferred hanging out with her

family, honestly."

"That's big," she said. Her eyebrow now raised in intrigue.

"Yeah, a lot has changed since we last spoke."

"Good changes though, I can see it on your face." I chuckled and Steve walked in the room looking like he wanted answers.

He stood still just inside the threshold of the door, both palms at his side facing the sky, lifting his chin as he spoke, "Bruh?"

"I'm good, man," I laughed.

He double pointed in my direction, "Bruh!"

"She's dope, right?" I asked, still laughing.

"Bruh," he said lifting his right fist in solidarity.

"I'm doing my best to keep it together, Steve."

"I'll tell you the story later, baby,"

Sabrina replied.

Steve hugged me and wished me a Happy New Year and told me where to find Jax and Dr. Chris. I walked into the family room to find the two of them chatting it up. Jax was telling her all about what Santa brought him on Christmas morning before he turned to greet me.

"Hi, Mr. Charlie!"

"Hey buddy!"

———

We hung out with Steve & Sabrina after the party was done and they thanked us for helping to serve the guests and run some of the games.

"So what's next for you two?" Sabrina asked. Dr. Chris glanced in my direction.

"One day at a time, Sabrina. We're taking it one day at a time," I said while lightly caressing Dr. Chris' back as we sat on their couch.

"Charlie, I remember at dinner the night that Jax broke his arm, you told him that

you wouldn't bring anybody here unless…"
Sabrina needled me.

"YEP! I remember what you're talking about," I said as I interrupted her mid-sentence, hoping to muffle the rest of her statement.

It didn't stop her from continuing, "So, you're telling me…"

"Yes. I'm telling you, yes."

She threw up both hands in resignation and laughed, "I'll drop it."

"You don't have to drop it. She already knows how I feel about her. My granddad called her my bride while he prayed over Christmas breakfast."

"Oh grand-pop, boxing you in," Steve said.

Dr. Chris laughed, "It wasn't anything we hadn't acknowledged with each other already, but they didn't know that at the time."

Sabrina asked Dr. Chris something

about spending time away from home on Christmas and I was caught off guard by her reply. "Charlie is home, so I was right where I wanted to be."

"Well there you have it folks," Steve said as I tried to hide my elation around my brother.

"So let me ask you about Jax's, checkup, Dr. Chris. I had a feeling that you knew Charlie when you walked in the room."

"Yeah, I did. But I couldn't figure out how he ended up in the room with Jax."

"That was all Steve's doing," Sabrina shared with a chuckle of disbelief.

I turned to Steve, "You told me that was Sabrina!"

"Threw me under the bus, huh?" she chuckled, looking in Steve's direction.

"I knew he wouldn't do it unless he thought you were on board, and look at where we ended up," he said opening his arms to all of us.

The sun was starting to set in the sky and two things were true. One, we had stayed so long at Steve and Sabrina's that the date I had planned just went flying out the window. Two, I hadn't made my New Year's promise yet. Between the two of those things I knew it was time for us to go. There was no way I was doing the latter in front of them. That was a private conversation for just the two of us.

I drove us back to Dr. Chris' condo and we had the chance to chat, alone, about the last couple of days, which were pretty busy.

I asked her directly, and it turns out she wasn't a fan of New Year's resolutions, but she did mention that she was a fan of picking a focus for the year ahead of her. I shared with her that I did the same thing but in the form of a promise to myself. I asked if she wanted to set a New Year's promise together and the idea seemed to go over well. So we brainstormed all that could be. Eventually we decided that we wanted to try something new together each month. So we set the wheels in motion, much like we had with our Spoonful of Sugarplums list for Christmas. I set up another checklist for our phones and we added items that might

be fun to tackle together.
- Try a new restaurant.
- Travel.
- Go horseback riding.
- Eat lunch on a blanket in the park.
- Conquer a ropes course.
- Go to a concert together.
- Visit family.
- Host a small gathering for friends.
- Adopt a Family (at Christmas).
- Attend a costume party together.
- Deliver food to a stranger.
- Go zip-lining.

We had our list, plus the remaining items from our yet to be completed Sugarplums list. I was looking forward to sharing the coming year with my heart and I had a feeling from the look on her face that she was looking forward to the year ahead as well.

CHAPTER 6

SCHOOL'S IN

Dr. Chris:

Charlie's school was set to be back in session on January 6th which only left us with a handful of days where he was free to roam about whenever. Lunch during the week, staying up in the evenings, random trips to the store for nothing in particular, following his heart wherever it led him; life was so beautiful while we were by each other's side. No rules, no assignments. Just the two of us feeling each other out and dancing along to the music we created together. He was so free and uninhibited.

We'd had a full two weeks since our first date and with the exception of December 23rd, he and I had spoken to or seen each other every day. I can't speak for him, but I was pretty much a lost cause. I would finish a day of work and the first person I'd call on my way home was Charlie. We'd figure out together whether or not he was meeting me at my condo or I was heading to his house for dinner.

On the 3rd of January, a Friday, he brought me lunch knowing that I had an early morning surgery on my schedule. He didn't stay to eat with me, just dropped it off and let me know that he was thinking about me. I knew days like that would be few and far between as time marched on. Because he was an educator, there just weren't many, if any, opportunities for him to steal away in the middle of the day to visit or even let me know that he was thinking about me. So I absorbed that moment, knowing that it likely wouldn't show up again until Spring Break at the very earliest.

Filled with gratitude, I unpacked my surprise lunch from the tote and noticed a note hanging out in the bottom of the bag. I reached in and lifted it towards my eyes as I took a bite of the chicken salad sandwich that Charlie packed. I felt the weight of a small object fall from its temporary home inside the note. I opened the note to read it, not paying attention to what had fallen.

"Hey Sugarplum, I'll be finishing up my lesson plans around the same time you're scheduled to finish your shift. Use this to let yourself in. I already have dinner plans prepared. Love, Charlie"

Use what now?

I fished into the bottom of the bag and pulled out the small object that fell from the letter; a house key. I assumed it was just a spare until I turned it over and saw my name engraved on it. Two weeks into dating and he gave me a key to his house. Did that mean I needed to give him a key to the condo? I was confused on what the protocol was for something like this. I've never given someone a key before. Shoot, I've never received a key before. My anxiety wanted to give it back but I didn't want him to think I had changed my mind about him.

I found my way down to my car once my shift had ended. I sent him a text to let him know I was on my way instead of calling since his note said that he would be focused on his lesson plans. He was only about a ten minute drive from the hospital, so I didn't have too far to go. When I arrived, I pulled into the driveway beside Chief and greeted him on my way to the front door, fiddling with the key that was in my pocket. I didn't see Charlie, so I decided to go ahead and use the key he had gifted me. I slowly unlocked the deadbolt then moved to the doorknob, pushing the door open as I twisted the lock to neutral. I didn't see him in his office, so I called his name to let him know I was in the house.

"Charlie?" There was no reply. I walked towards the living room. Nothing. "Charlie?" I paused to listen and see if I could hear him somewhere in the house. I walked into the kitchen. No Charlie. I walked to the bathroom on the main level. No Charlie. I walked upstairs, calling his name again. No response and no Charlie. Where was he? I pulled out my phone to call him and see what was going on when my phone rang. Of course it was Charlie.

"Charlie?" I asked, wondering why I was in his empty house.

"Hey Sugarplum! Did you make it inside okay?"

I was pointed, "I did, but where are you?"

His reply was gentle, "I'm on my way now."

"I'm confused. Help me out here."

He spoke methodically, "I'm on my way. I'll explain it when I get there."

Still puzzled, I tried to make sense of the situation in my mind, "Do you want me to come back?"

"No, stay there. I'm almost home."

My soul smiled hearing him tell me that he was almost home.

"You know where everything is," he finished.

"Do you need me to get anything started in the kitchen?"

His voice sounded muffled, like it was off in the distance, "Her heart is so big. She just asked me if I needed her to start anything in the kitchen."

"Charlie?"

"Yes, Dr. Chris? I mean, no, I'm almost home. I got us."

I remembered my prayer that I always see Charlie's actions for what they were and not with my own filter and I leaned heavily on it in this moment, because I know I heard another woman's voice reply to his comment about me, and it wasn't Sabrina.

I accepted it for what it was and stopped myself from reading into things, "Okay. I'm going to grab something to drink and plop down on the couch."

"Sounds good, beautiful. There's some fresh juice in the fridge if you want it." There he was, my sweet guy.

"Thank you, Charlie."

"Of course. You know I'll always take care of you. I'll see you in a few minutes okay?" his steadfast resolve affirmed my faith in him.

"Okay. Be careful."

"Roger that. I love you."

"I love you."

I heard the car door close as he got home, but I didn't think to see who was dropping him off. Wait, let me tell the truth. I thought about it, but decided that I didn't want to see. I'd rather he just tell me. The key was in the deadbolt. Murder, She Wrote was on tv and Jessica was just about to crack another murder case. I didn't understand how they could say that WE were the violent ones and here she was trying to solve a new murder in the same small Maine town every single week. Charlie opened the door just as the alleged murderer tried to snuff out Jessica on the show before she could pin him to the crime. Needless to say, I jumped when the front door opened.

I had my hand over my heart when Charlie walked into the living room with flowers, his messenger bag, a bag of Chinese takeout, and a broad smile. I loved the way he loved me.

I stood to greet him, glad he wasn't some murderer coming to stop me from turning him over to the authorities, "Hi Charlie!"

He hugged me, the bag of takeout swinging like a pendulum behind me, "Hey, Sugarplum!" I closed my eyes as he achingly kissed me, like he had missed me or something.

I pulled my face back slowly, and looked him squarely in his eyes, "Hmmm."

"Too much?" he asked.

My heart raced as I teased him with my words, "I almost pulled you upstairs."

"No, we decided that we were going to wait." He was adamant about sticking to our promise, such an endearing word.

"We did," I said. "You know I was kidding."

"Do I?" he laughed.

I offered him a quick peck on his cheek, "You do. Can I grab something from you?" I asked, still standing close enough to feel his breath.

"Sure. These are for you," he said handing me the bouquet of light red carnations.

"Thank you, Charlie. What are these for?"

"Smiles, that's all. Just thinking about you today and I wanted to celebrate you and thank you for helping me open my eyes and see the world around me."

I didn't have any words. I just shook my head at him and bashfully smiled. "Charlie."

"I know, I didn't have to get you flowers."

"Yep."

"But maybe I wanted to see your face light up. Maybe I wanted to love you right. I just want you to know where my heart is, Chris. Always."

"Thank you, sweetheart."

He raised the bag of food, "Are you hungry? Shall we eat?"

"Yes, and yes."

"Okay, give me a second to get this set up in the dining room."

"Sure. Do you have a vase or a jar that I can put these in?"

"I have a big mason jar, will that work?"

"Yep!"

"2nd shelf from the top in the pantry."

"Okay, I'll grab it after I turn off the tv."

I paused for 30 seconds or so, watching as Jessica turned over all her evidence to the police. Just as they cuffed the murderer, the doorbell rang.

"Charlie are you expecting company?"

"No. Can you see who it is?"

I turned off the tv and walked to the front door, there was a woman on the other side, about my height and possible around the same age as me. I opened the door and greeted her.

"Hi! You must be Chris."

"Maybe?"

"I'm Charlie's co-worker, Jessica."

"Hi Jessica, would you like to come in while I grab Charlie?"

"No, just give him this," she handed me his phone. "Tell him it fell between the car seat and the center console in my car."

"I'll do that. Are you sure you don't want to come inside? I can grab him really quickly."

"No need! Just tell him I said I'll see him on Monday."

"I'll do that."

"Also, you are so brave! Going to meet his parents after only a few days of knowing him. I don't know that I would have said yes."

"Umm, thank you? I think."

She laughed. I was not amused. "So nice to meet you. Hope to see you at the MLK program that we're planning!"

"Time will tell."

"Have a good night, girl!"

"Alright. You too, Jessica."

Oh my, I had gone from watching a nosy Jessica on tv, to meeting a nosy Jessica in real life. They were giving everyone named Jessica a bad name!

Charlie came in the entryway just as I had closed the door holding his phone in one hand and the flowers in the other.

"Who was at the door? Oh, she found it!"

"She said it was between the seat and the center console."

"The one place I couldn't get my hand between to search."

"She asked me if I was going to attend that MLK program that the two of you were planning."

"Yeah, I was hoping to tell you more about that over dinner."

"Were you also going to tell me that you spilled the beans about our entire relationship to her?" I said chuckling.

"She asked what I had been up to over the break and I told her that I met my bride. When she asked for details I just filled in the blanks."

"So I see!"

"I'm sorry Chris. I didn't mean to put you in an awkward spot. I just got excited to tell somebody about our relationship!"

He was so cute. I kissed him on the cheek and told him that I was going to get a mason jar for the flowers. He pulled one from behind his back like some sort of magic act. I'm not sure where it was hiding or how, but I thanked him for it and took the flowers into the kitchen to prepare them for display. He followed me in there.

"Do you think we're going to be okay?"

"Oh, Charlie, we're fine. Just be prepared for all the teachers to know your business when you go back to school on Monday," I chuckled.

"Do you really think she's going to tell everyone else?"

"If she felt comfortable enough to tell me about my relationship 20 seconds after meeting me, she's going to tell people she's worked with for at least 6 months and hasn't seen for 3 weeks. That's probably already happened."

"Oh no."

I laughed at his reaction. He looked like he was dreading their responses.

"I mean, maybe I'm wrong Charlie. You know Jessica better than I do."

He grabbed some plates and silverware and took them to the dining room table while I filled the jar with water. He came back in and kissed my temple, apologizing again for sharing all the details with Jessica. I assured him that it was okay and the two of us moved into the dining room for dinner.

This was the first night that it felt like we had settled into a relationship groove. I'm not sure if it was the fact that I had a key and he trusted me to let myself into his house while he wasn't here, or if it was him bringing dinner home for us, or if it was a combination of those things in addition to us working through what could potentially have been a point of conflict. Either way, this felt natural, and that slightly terrified me.

———

Charlie:

She looked comfortable but I was having a hard time placing the other emotion that was written all over her face. I had tried to convince her that she didn't have anything to worry about when I realized that the entire act of convincing someone of something seemed kind of manipulative. Instead I decided that I'd just speak the truth and let it go.

I asked how the rest of her day was and listened as she spoke, between bites of black pepper chicken, about how her patients were all progressing. She and I had settled into a natural groove. I knew there was no way I'd be able to make it back to the house by the time she reached me, so I had a key made for her. I honestly didn't think twice about it because I knew, long term, what

I wanted. The look that was on her face though, made me wonder if it was moving too fast for her.

"Dr. Chris,"

"Yes, Charlie?"

"I'm sorry I wasn't here when you came over."

"It's okay, Charlie. I mean, I had a key," she smiled.

"You did. Was that okay?" I asked, watching to see if she would tell me the complete truth or half of one.

"It was unexpected, that's for sure."

Complete truth.

"I mean, I can take it back if it's too soon for you."

"No need to take it back. I'd just rather you be here when I'm coming over is all."

"That I can do," I said with a smile.

"What made you decide to give me a key, Charlie?"

"I'm an open book, Chris. I'm not interested in limiting your access to me."

"Are you always like this in relationships? Or, I mean were you?"

"An open book? Yes. Unlimited access? No."

"So how many keys are walking around to this door, Charlie?"

"Three." She raised an eyebrow in search of an answer. "Your key, my key, and the key that I gave Steve & Sabrina in case of emergencies." Her face softened as she gazed in my eyes.

"Have you ever given someone a key to your place before?"

"Never."

"Oh wow."

"Yep. I don't even know who I am right now," I said through a nervous chuckle.

I was only half joking there. I had morphed into a more responsible, more caring version of myself in spite of my last heartbreak. I had a resounding sense of calm that I would be okay. "See what you've done to me woman?"

"Charlie, I've never given nor received a key before, so I wasn't sure what to do with that new experience."

"I think we're going to stumble into a lot of firsts together."

"Yeah, I think so," she nervously laughed. I reached across the table to hold her hand and caressed her fingers. In the background, Spotify was playing some music they thought we'd like to hear.

"How are you feeling right now?" I asked her.

"I'm okay, just a little internal battle with my fears is all."

Emily King sang to us as we sat in acknowledgment of the work we'd need to put in to make this work. "There's a side of you, needs to be afraid. There's a side of me, makes it all okay."

We looked at each other and smiled through it all. Music had a way of providing the two of us with the answers we needed to keep moving forward.

"So tell me about this program you're planning," she asked me.

———

The day had arrived, January 20th. All of the early morning practices with the kiddos had made for some long tiresome days. But Dr. Chris was there in the evenings, encouraging me to keep pushing. She didn't complain about the nights I had to go to bed early because of a pre-dawn wake up time the following day. She simply accepted it as is. She didn't question why I had fallen asleep during movie nights. Instead she held my head in her lap or rubbed my back as I slept. She was extraordinarily caring and I knew that once this was all over, I wanted to return the favor for the support she had provided me.

She was supposed to be coming straight from work but the auditorium was filling up and I hadn't seen her yet. I was peering out into the audience from backstage like all the kids who were trying to see their parents.

"Do you see her yet?" one of my students asked patting me on my back. I turned around to find Joel shaking his head and looking up at me like he was hoping the answer was yes. I must have looked distressed for him to come check on me like that. I was starting to think Joel felt as invested in my relationship as I did after seeing the two of us in the carriage on the Plaza.

"Not yet, Joel, but I tell you what buddy, I think they're getting everybody in order back there. Make sure they find you and I'll let you know when she gets here."

He nodded and galloped his way to the back where Jessica was placing students in program order. He stopped at her, pointed in my direction, shook his head and gave her an update. Turns out Joel was a pawn. Jessica had asked him to check. The same thing happened in the teacher's lounge the first day back from break. Dr. Chris was right. Jessica had told everyone all of our business before I could even step foot in the building. All the teachers cheered when I arrived and I knew exactly why. All but one of them had previously attempted to set me up on a date with someone they knew. I declined all of their requests. I know they were happy that I found someone, but why on earth she felt it was her responsibility to let everyone know was beyond me.

She was wrong for that one, and I attempted to set some clear boundaries with her. Apparently though, she didn't understand the word, boundaries. This was far beyond crossing the line. I made a mental note to talk to her about using students to dig for personal information but almost lost my train of thought when I saw her. She must have gone home to change. I know she wouldn't wear a dress to the hospital.

I watched her walk across the multipurpose room. Her long legged strides taking her to a seat in the back of the hall, slightly behind a pillar. There was an open, unobstructed seat further down the back row, but knowing Dr. Chris, she probably chose to leave that seat open for a parent or relative of a student who was in the show. As she sat alone and reviewed her program, I sent her a quick text.

"You look stunning, Dr. Chris"

I watched a smile peel across her face while she craned her neck in search of me. She looked to her left and right, in the front and rear of the room. I knew she wouldn't be able to find me where I was standing. I had successfully tucked myself behind one of the curtains, stage right. She sent me a reply.

"Thank you, Charlie!"

"Ur welcome, Sugarplum"

She started her search again and I waited until her face turned in my direction before stepping out where she could see me. We locked eyes and held each others gaze until she decided to send me a text.

"Hey there, handsome"

I read the text and tried to hide my smile before refocusing my eyes on her and lifting my phone to my heart.

"Thx for coming"

She mouthed her reply, "Of course."

Before I knew it, there was a little hand tapping my back. I turned around to find Joel, who saw me miming to Dr. Chris from his spot at the back of the line. He peeked out from around me and waved to her. I escorted him back to his place in line and gave the kiddos a quick pep talk before walking out to emcee the show. I was so proud of all of them for their hard work. They did a fantastic job, just as I knew they would. I waited until they were all reunited with their parents before I found my way to Dr. Chris, who was chatting with Jessica.

I interrupted Jessica mid-sentence to embrace my love.

"They did great, Charlie!" Dr. Chris gushed.

"Didn't they?" I asked.

"I was just telling Jessica that the two of you did a great job of adding meaning to this holiday."

"Thanks, Dr. Chris," Jessica started. "I'll leave the two of you to yourselves."

I nodded and kept my attention focused

on the woman who had come to watch 50 elementary school students, only one of whom she knew, give a presentation about Dr. King. I thanked her for the support and asked if she was hungry. She told me that she had plans for dinner, which I assumed didn't include me so I scrunched up my face.

"I got us," she told me. "Follow behind me?"

"Yep, let me grab my bag and we can go." I went backstage to grab my messenger bag and found Jessica on the phone with someone, telling them how Dr. Chris had shown up to the program. That was all the reminder I needed to have a more specific conversation about boundaries.

I cleared my throat so she knew I was there, and waited until she got off the phone before asking who she was flapping her gums to now. No, I didn't use those words. I had more tact than that. But that was the gist of the message. When she stuttered through her response I asked why my business was so important to her that she thought it appropriate to use a student to spy. No coherent reply, again.

"What I do in my spare time has no bearings on your life." She stood still, waiting for me to say something else to make her feel better. I didn't have anything else to say.

"I'm sorry, Charlie," she said, looking at the floor, "I'll leave it alone."

"Thank you," I said, hoping she was done.

I grabbed my messenger bag and turned around to see Dr. Chris chatting with Joel and his mom. I smiled watching her stoop down, dress and all, to chat with Joel face-to-face. Curious about their conversation, but mostly just hungry, I found my way to the back of the auditorium to join them.

"Hi Mr. Hughes!" Joel shouted. "Your girlfriend is really nice!"

"Isn't she Joel? You did great tonight buddy." I replied, shifting the conversation, or at least trying to.

"She's really pretty too!" he added.

"Joel!" his mom said, sounding

embarrassed.

"I'm just trying to keep up with your mom," Dr. Chris added.

"That's pretty much impossible," Joel finished which gave us all a good laugh.

"Thank you for your work, Mr. Hughes," his mom said, hoping to shift the conversation once more.

"You got it. I'm looking forward to the next program." I turned towards Dr. Chris. "Are you ready my dear?" She nodded and we excused ourselves to the hallway then down to my classroom.

"Charlie, this was great. Thank you for inviting me."

"Thank you for coming. It meant a lot to me to look out and see you in the audience." "I wouldn't miss it."

I gave her the rundown on Jessica using Joel and how I tried to set some boundaries again. She shrugged and shook her head.

"Nothing you can do to stop her Charlie.

Just let it go." I nodded, understanding that she was right.

She glanced at her watch. "So let's talk about those dinner plans, mister."

I looked up at the clock on the wall. "It is getting late. Let's go. Wait, where are we going?"

"You're following me remember?"

"Right. Right." I trailed behind her on the way to the parking lot, helped her into her car, then hustled to my truck and followed her around through the neighborhoods in our respective vehicles. I had no idea where we were going. Then she took a familiar right hand turn and we ended up in our neighborhood, my neighborhood. She pulled into the driveway and parked in her spot. Slightly confused I hopped out of the truck and opened her car door to help her out.

"What are we doing here?" I asked her.

"Having dinner, Charlie."

She took my hand and I led her to the

front door, unlocking it and letting her in first. Something smelled great. "Did you leave something on the stove Charlie?"

"Uhh, no. I didn't."

"Oh that's right. I used the magic key earlier today."

I drew her close to me so I could kiss her temple and hold her near my heart.

"Stethoscope."

She giggled, took my coat off and hung it in the coat closet, then led me by the hand into the dining room where she asked me to have a seat at the head of the table. There were two place settings, the second was seated immediately to my left - heart side. I wanted to go in the kitchen to help her, but she reminded me that she had dinner tonight.

"I got us, remember?" she asked as she turned on some soft music and slipped away into the kitchen. She returned wearing an apron. Her pot-holder covered hands carrying the ceramic liner of a slow cooker. The lid covering its contents was foggy, but the scent that was wafting out was enough to make my stomach howl. She sat the ceramic insert on the trivet that was in front of us and retreated to the kitchen once more. When she returned this time she was carrying a bamboo salad bowl and a pitcher of juice.

"When did you have time to do all of this?" I asked as she disappeared into the kitchen again.

Coming back out with a carving knife and the only salad dressing that was in my fridge she replied, "I picked up the ingredients on the way home and threw everything in the slow cooker before taking a quick shower and heading to the school."

My head cocked sideways, "You showered here?"

Looking slightly embarrassed she replied, "Yes, was that okay?"

I was glad she felt comfortable enough to do so. "Of course, but I didn't think you had anything here for a shower," I said.

She smiled slyly, "I do now. I've been

planning this surprise for a while, Charlie. I saw how hard you were working to ensure that the program was good and I wanted to celebrate you. So I had some extra toiletries delivered to the condo so I could pack it in a bag and bring it here after my shift today."

"You sneaky woman!" I said in jest. Right on cue a timer went off in the kitchen and Dr. Chris disappeared once more. This time she came out without the apron but with a plate of her homemade cornbread muffins and what looked to be honey-butter.

"I don't understand how you had the time to do all of this today."

"Never underestimate the power of a determined woman, Charlie."

"I see! Well, shall we pray?" I asked, as she bowed her head in response. I prayed over the food as normal and added a special prayer of thanks for allowing us the time and opportunity to celebrate our one-month anniversary.

"Amen" she said as she squeezed my hand, in much the same manner as she had when we prayed together on our 2nd date.

"Charlie-" she said, sounding surprised and a bit taken aback.

"Yes, I remembered, Sugarplum." She unveiled a whole chicken that had been roasting in the slow cooker since she got 'home.' Every single time I didn't think I could possibly love her more than I did, she did something that was naturally her and my love grew deeper still.

I didn't expect for her to take the lead on our anniversary celebration, but I so appreciated it after the extra work that went into preparing for the school program. Our conversations over dinner were completely random in nature, which only added to my deepening love for her.

After we were finished eating we took those random conversations into the kitchen and washed the dishes together. I had been holding in my emotions to the best of my ability but I couldn't take it any longer. While my limbs were forearm deep in sudsy water and Dr. Chris was drying dishes, I leaned over and kissed her. The plate she was wiping dry fell from her hands and I somehow caught it while still lip locked, and placed it back in the suds. She broke from our kiss, used the dish towel to dry my hands and arms, and draped it over the sink. The two of us held onto each other and slow danced around the kitchen while the faint sound of Mali Music playing in the dining room kept count. I sang along.

> *"There's nowhere else to go*
> *There's nowhere else to be*
> *Than here in love with you*
> *You know what's the best for me*
> *...*
> *That's why I'll always be in love with you*
> *Still, through it all*
> *That's when we're going up, we're going up*
> *When we rise and fall*
> *You know I'll always be in love with you*
> *Still..."*

I looked into her eyes as I sang, feeling each and every lyric. My Heart got the best of me today and I so deeply appreciated her.

"I made your bed after I took a shower this afternoon, sweetheart," she said biting her lower lip. I made the bed everyday and wasn't entirely sure what she meant. Then

I remembered our visit to Mom and Dad's for Christmas.

"Two separate sleeping spaces?" I asked. She grinned and I nodded. I sweetly kissed her on the temple and placed my cheek against her forehead as we danced out of the kitchen, through the dining room, and over to the staircase where I intertwined my fingers with hers and led her upstairs to the master bedroom.

CHAPTER 7

VALENTINE'S DAY

Just three weeks after we celebrated our one month anniversary, Valentine's Day snuck up on us. In those three weeks our relationship continued to advance at an exponential pace.

There wasn't a day that we had not seen each other, including the days where I worked a double shift. Charlie found his way to the hospital to drop off some food or a cider with sugarplums so I wouldn't have to think twice about how to stay well nourished while I was busy serving others.

There were weeknights when we would sit and chat for hours on end about nothing, and weekends where we would veg out and hold themed movie streaming marathons similar to the one we had during the snowstorm that trapped us together. He had arranged an opportunity for the two of us to spend an afternoon at a food kitchen serving those who were in need, after which the two of us vowed to repeat it at least once a month together. We had even ventured out for a couple of fancy "date night" dinners, but the truth of the matter is there was nothing like doing nothing with Charlie. It had become the thing I most looked forward to. Even after a "date night" out, I was ready to snuggle up next to him on the couch or just chill together, me reading and him scrolling through his social media feeds, or vice versa. He was nothing short of a rock as I navigated through my own nervous hang-ups about our relationship moving so fast.

He didn't have to do anything except be present and consistent, which was more of a gift than he knew. So in my mind, I wasn't expecting much to be different for Valentine's Day because I felt like he did such a great job of celebrating and honoring me each and every day.

Marlo and I had found time to video chat every couple of weeks. Our conversations held two-fold importance, one - so he could update me on his move to Colorado, and two - so he could make sure that I wasn't blocking myself from the "love of a lifetime," as he called it. We checked in with each other two days before Valentine's Day and he asked what our plans were for the day. I honestly had no clue.

"What is expected of the woman on Valentine's Day, Marlo?"

"Well, my date has told me that she has a gift for me, but I really feel like it's more my place to provide the romance."

"Yeah? Wait. Date? Speak." He laughed and told me all about how quickly it happened.

"I kept thinking there was no way this was actually happening, that something was going to go terribly wrong. But nope. This is happening."

"Aww friend, I'm so excited for you!" I said, hearing Chief rumble into the driveway and the driver's door close. "So Charlie is just getting home," I told Marlo.

"Wait aren't you in his house?" he

asked, his face all scrunched together.

"I am," I said straight faced and very matter of fact as I heard his key opening the front door.

"Did he run an errand or something? I mean you're just there by yourself?"

"I was. He's home now," I said tilting my head back to give him a kiss as he entered the room. "Hey sweetheart."

"Hey Sugarplum," Charlie said, gazing down into my eyes. He glanced over to my tablet and waved, "Hi Marlo!"

"Charlie, you just left this woman in your space by herself?"

"She has a key! She can come and go whenever she wants," Charlie said as he dropped his keys on his key hook and walked towards the office where his landline resided.

Marlo's mouth was open wide enough that you would've thought I was doing a remote dental check-up.

"Y'all are on another level of comfort

with each other." I slowly nodded as Charlie chuckled from the other room. "I can't talk to you when you're grinning like that, Chris. Go be with your husband, ma'am!"

"Wait, you're not gonna tell me about your Valentine?"

"Next time. Matter of fact, we'll be in Kansas City in a couple of weeks. Let's make sure we all connect then."

"What's her name?"

"I'll text you. BYE CHARLIE!" he hollered.

Charlie leaned out from his office and waved, just as I moved the tablet so Marlo could see him, "Be easy, Marlo!" By the time I had repositioned the tablet back in front of my face to say goodbye, Marlo had already ended the chat.

I closed my tablet and asked Charlie about his day, then listened as he told me all about his students' progress. The conversation shifted naturally into school Valentine's Day plans and eventually I asked for Charlie's thoughts on our Valentine's

Day plans. He smiled and changed the subject. "So, Marlo is seeing someone?"

"It sounds like it. He was just about to share some more details when I told him that you were here," I said, rising from the couch and walking in his direction.

"My bad."

"Don't do that. So about Valentine's Day, Charlie?" I asked from the doorway of his office.

"Don't worry about Valentine's Day, Chris," he said with an ornery smile.

"What does that mean?"

"It means, I got us," he said without so much as a glance in my direction.

"Charlie, that doesn't help me know what to do for you."

He rose from the chair behind the desk and stood in front of me, holding my shoulders. "You don't have to do anything for me on Valentine's Day."

"Okay Charlie," I said, knowing good and well that's not what was about to happen.

"I got us," he said once more as I lifted my hands and pretended like I was washing them.

———

Valentine's Day arrived and Charlie woke up excited. He left me a voicemail bright and early, "Good-morning, beautiful! Happy Valentine's Day! I left a little something for you in your fridge before I left last night. Start there when you get up. It will tell you what's next. I love you, Sugarplum. Have a great day. I'm looking forward to seeing you this evening."

I'm not sure how he was able to leave a voicemail without calling, but he found a way. His excitement stirred a fire within me. I found myself running to the refrigerator instead of patiently finding my way there throughout the natural course of my morning. I suddenly had a feeling that the gift I had prepared for him was about to pale in comparison to the experience he had likely set up for me.

I opened the door to the fridge and at first glance nothing seemed out of the ordinary. As I was closing the door I noticed a tumbler with my name on it. I lifted it from the shelf and could tell that something was inside. I slowly unscrewed the lid to find a cup full of fresh juice with a familiar scent. It smelled like the Sweet Potato Pie juice recipe that I loved so much. I closed my eyes, slowly tilted the cup back and took a sip. It was perfect! Charlie had found my favorite recipe and recreated it. If this was any indication of what I was about to receive all day, I had a feeling I'd be crying sentimental tears by the day's end.

On the backside of the cup there was a sticky note. I pulled it off and read its message,

"Your favorite, to start the day off right. In your closet, a new outfit to wear tonight."

I took my personalized tumbler and juice on a walk down the hallway and back to the bedroom to take a peek in the closet. I steadied my feet, took a minute and slowly opened the door to the walk-in. How on earth was I going to find something unique in a sea of clothing? Tucked high up on the shelf was a box with a bow.

I set my drink on a shelf so I could pull the box down without throwing off my balance. A sticky note on the top of the box read,

"My love can only warm so much
These should add a softer touch"

I opened the box to find a new hoodie (I had built quite the collection) and some fleece lined sweatpants. Tucked inside the hoodie was a pair of thick cabin socks and on the socks, another note.

"For after work, tonight and more
Don't forget to check your drawer"

I shook my head and carried the box into the bedroom, sitting it on the end of my bed before slipping back in the closet to grab my juice and turn off the light. Keeping an eye on the time, I opened my sock drawer where there were 3 more pairs of cabin socks waiting for me. There was a sticky note standing up between one of the pairs. I grabbed it as a fleeting thought hit me. *How on earth did he pull this off?*

"Right now I know you're wondering how.
I'll never tell. Not later. Not now.
Your coat has the next clue"

I got cleaned up and dressed for work and grabbed my new tumbler and my keys before heading to the coat closet in the entryway. I walked past the table that used to hold the honeysuckle stems from our first date and noticed that they had been replaced with a vase filled with purple hydrangeas, a single honeysuckle stem, and peppered with light red carnations. I knew the connection of the honeysuckle and the carnations, but I made a mental note to look up information about hydrangeas before I saw him that evening.

I took a picture of the flowers and sent it to him with a message that said, "Thank you," and then I wondered where my honeysuckle stems had gone. They were still alive yesterday and now they were gone.

I opened the closet to grab my coat so I could head to work and I noticed a sticky note on the back of the door.

"You walked right past them"

I backed up and walked into the living room again, taking a quick scan of the room. There, on top of the console table near the window was a planter filled with dirt and the honeysuckle stems from our first date which had started to root in January. And on the planter? Another note, of course.

"I can't work miracles, but these grew new chutes,
  They'll grow stronger still, when we plant some roots

I know you love these too much to just get rid of them - don't forget your coat."

I stared at the note getting misty eyed. It was like he was reading my mind. I always wondered how couples who had been together for a while could know what each other was thinking. That type of synergy seemed like a carrot on a stick until I met Charlie. I hustled back to the coat closet before I fell behind on time and tossed on my coat, then ran back in the bedroom and packed my new sweats and a pair of cabin socks in the overnight bag with Charlie's gift. Then back to the entryway to grab my keys and tumbler which I had left on the table. I dropped the keys in my coat pocket and felt another note. *What are you doing, Charlie?*

"Yep another note for you - be safe
Check your windshield before you drive."

When I got down to my car, I saw another carnation tucked underneath the wiper and placed it on the passenger seat before heading off to work.

At some point during my drive, Charlie replied to my text. I noticed it after getting settled in at the hospital.

"I love your smile."

I looked at the picture I'd sent with my last text. There it was again, a reflection of me smiling in the glass of the picture hanging above the bouquet of flowers that Charlie had given me. I replied to his text with the extreme smiling emoji. I didn't know what else was up his sleeve but I had a feeling something else was on the way.

The morning and afternoon were both scheduled to be busy, so I wasn't sure how

I was going to work lunch into this day. Fortunately for me I didn't have to wait too long to figure that out. Around 11:30, when his class was eating lunch, Charlie sent another message.

"Lunch is being delivered to you and your wing at noon."

"Like the hospital staff?"

"Yes ma'am. Happy Valentine's Day!"

At two minutes before noon, the delivery from The Fresh Pantry had arrived. Our team was beyond excited to have lunch delivered to them. I waited until they all had the chance to grab some food before I stepped in to get lunch. I wasn't sure what was going to be left, as I watched the boxed lunches dwindle down to near nothing. But there were two boxes left when I got there; one small and one large. They both had Charlie's handwriting on them. The smaller of the boxes read, "Thanks for all you do!" The larger of the two held a special message.

"For my Love, Dr. Chris"

I held it in my hands and stared at it,

wondering how he had the time to do all of this. The nurses had gushingly gathered around me.

"Did Charlie buy lunch for all of us?"

"I think so!" I told them, standing completely befuddled. "I had no idea this was coming. I'm just as surprised as you."

"Dr. Chris, you never did tell us how the two of you met!" Susan said.

I smiled knowing she wouldn't believe me and continued anyway, "We told you the truth. I had literally just met him a few days before he came to the Jubilee with me to play Santa."

"That story again," they all laughed.

"Really, I bumped into him at the Fresh Grind coffeehouse," just as I said it, a familiar face stepped off the elevator.

"Dr. Chris?"

I said what was on my mind, "Oakley! Hi. What are you doing here?"

"Charlie called in a delivery for 'A Cider with a Spoonful of Sugarplums' to be delivered to you here."

"Oh. I'm sorry if this is awkward."

"Nonsense. When I saw the order, I knew that I needed to handle it to make sure that it actually got delivered to you. Our regular delivery driver is out today and I didn't trust this one with the backup."

"You didn't have to do that."

"I did. Plus, I owed you an apology anyway. I feel like my actions may have caused some tension when the two of you started dating. I was in a pretty selfish place. I'm sorry for that."

I didn't know what to say. She was right. Her actions did cause some tension in our relationship, but it helped Charlie place a stake in the ground and build trust early. In some sense, it helped to bring the two of us closer, faster. I hugged her and wished her a Happy Valentine's Day and she handed me his handwritten sticky note.

"He loves you, girl," she said as she

turned around to leave before waving and wishing me a Happy Valentine's Day as the elevator doors closed.

"Who was that?" Susan asked.

"Charlie's ex."

Susan eyed me with caution, "Wait. His ex?"

"Mmm hmm."

Silence filled the gap between her thoughts and the statement that followed, "Don't drink that cider. She probably spit in it."

"For some reason, I don't think she did," I said while chuckling.

I looked at the note that Oakley had delivered,

"Refill your tumbler with our favorite hot drink,
Tonight we'll drink from glasses that clink.
(Relaxed and fancy-pants - check your other coat pocket before you leave work)

Love you, Sugarplum."

Time couldn't move fast enough that afternoon. Isn't that always the way it works when there's somewhere else you want to be? It's like the clocks had all decided they were going on break. I dove into my work, hoping it would help speed things up. I guess it worked. Before I knew it my shift was coming to an end and I was putting on my coat so I could get out of there. I reached into my left coat pocket to see what Charlie had left for me. I pulled out a new pair of gloves that held a note,

"You might need these. It's supposed to be chilly tonight."

I picked up the phone and called Charlie to let him know I was on my way home. He sounded excited to see me, but I don't think he was more excited than I was to see him. The care and consideration he poured into those gifts helped the anticipation build throughout the day. I did ask him about the gloves, but he wouldn't tell me anything except, "Bring them in the house with you when you get home."

So I did, along with my overnight bag. I

took my gift for him out of the bag before I went inside, hoping to gift it to him before I went to the bedroom to change clothes. I used my key to let myself in and hoped I would see him soon thereafter, but I didn't. His truck was outside, but I didn't see Charlie. I set his gift on the bottom step and hustled upstairs to the master bedroom. I heard him rustling around in the backyard as I was changing clothes and I nodded knowing exactly where to go once I was dressed.

By the time I got finished changing, I saw him standing at the bottom of the steps in some comfy looking sweats, with his gift box in hand.

"I didn't need anything, ma'am!"

"Charlie, it's the day of Love."

"I got us."

"I got you."

He grinned, "Well are you gonna come down here or not, lady?" I slowly descended the stairs to greet Charlie from the bottom step. He wrapped his arms around my waist and I held onto him like he was about to leave on a two-week trip.

"Are you ready for dinner?" he asked from within our embrace.

"After you open your gift." I was adamant about things flowing in that order.

He peered inside and grinned at the contents of the box, "Yep. You got me."

"Is it okay?"

"It's perfect."

"Now I'm ready for dinner," I said still smiling from his surprised expression.

He guided me outside to a bistro table underneath a patio heater, pulling out my chair and helping to scoot it in for me. In a move that I'd grown to expect from Charlie, he turned on a playlist that he had curated for the evening. I had not expected him to wheel out a lidded chrome food cart with our dinner hiding underneath. The two of us ate the dinner he had prepare on fancy china, with linen napkins, and drank juice from champagne flutes, while wearing our hoodies and sweatpants - completely relaxed and yet, still fancy pants. I also wore the gloves I had received from him, and he donned the scarf that he still had not returned from our cold first date.

"Chris, I wanted this Valentine's Day to be a reflection of just how loved I feel by you every day. We could get dressed up and be fancy, or we could be relaxed and comfortable with each other and my love would remain the same. Also, I hope you don't mind me planting the honeysuckle stems in dirt."

Too anxious to address his feelings, I opted only to respond to the latter statement. "Charlie, I love it. It's been ready to root."

"It has."

"I've been ready to root," I said.

Charlie held up the gift box he had received from me. "So I see!" he said, glancing at me in his signature, 'How did you get here' gaze. "Should we go watch a movie?"

"You didn't have one selected already?"

"It's your choice. We can watch whatever. I'll probably be watching you watch the tv anyway..."

I could feel my face growing flushed, "Charlie."

"...plotting how I'm going to sneak in a cuddle or a kiss," he said with a smirk.

"I can't take you anywhere."

"Well it's a good thing we're here then, huh?"

I had been bested in our game of wits. "I suppose so, Charlie."

"I love you, Sugarplum."

"It's a Rom-Com kind of night."

"Great! Let's load up the cart. I'll wheel our dishes back into the house, while you pick out the movies." Charlie said. "And there's already popcorn in there. It's not as good as yours, but I gave it my best shot."

And with that, my zero expectation Valentine's Day went down in the history books as one of my favorite days on record. As I studied this man walking around wearing his heart on his sleeve I came to realize that he loves me without the expectation of receiving love in return.

"I'm sure I'll love it just as much as I love you, Sweetheart."

CHAPTER 8

DOUBLE DATE

Valentine's Day was my chance to demonstrate my love in action. I wasn't expecting her to do the same for me, but I'm not sure why. I've seen how openly she loves her patients and her work family, and I had the chance to witness just how much she loves her family and mine. Her love of others was constantly on display. Even knowing that, I was still surprised on the day of love when she left a box at the bottom of my steps. I wanted her to feel my love, and I almost took away the opportunity for her to return the favor to me as well.

The fact that she went out of her way to gift me something, was enough for me to fall in love with her heart all over again.

"I got us," I told her, trying to reiterate that this day was about her.

She looked at me with conviction and caring resolve as she told me, "I got you." I just wanted to hold her in my arms and keep our love safe from the outside world. It truly didn't even matter what was inside the box at that point, but she wouldn't let me start dinner without opening it. I nearly went turn-turtle when I opened the gift. She already had me, but the amount of trust it took for her to give me a key to her condo meant that her head had caught up with her heart. That meant she was all in for us, that she saw our love as evergreen and not just some beautiful clippings that were going to eventually wilt away.

That was all the confidence I needed to put my next plan into motion. I knew she and I had already had the conversation about knowing what this relationship was, but things moved so swiftly that I didn't want to rush downstream only to have her capsize or jump overboard for fear of the current pushing her too fast. That would've had some unintended consequences. Now that she was in my life, I couldn't imagine experiencing life without her.

I called up Steve the day after Valentine's Day to update him on what he called my Crazy Valentine's Day Scheme.

"So you pulled it off?"

"I did man. Here's the thing though," I paused.

"Uh oh, what's that?" he asked, sounding a little worried.

I didn't know how else to describe it to him, "She got me."

He laughed heartily at my expense, "I mean obviously, if you were willing to do so much for her for just Valentine's Day."

"No." I hoped to correct him. "I mean, she surprised me with a gift."

"It's Valentine's Day, Charlie. Women get men gifts too!"

"Yeah, but I told her that I was going to take care of us."

"So you didn't want her to show you any love at all?" Steve asked, his voice laced with suspicion.

"She does that every day, man. I just wanted to give her a day that was all about her."

"That's what her birthday is for," he chuckled.

"Yeah, I have a plan for that too," I told him.

"So what, are you gonna propose to her?" he asked sounding slightly concerned.

"Yeah, with a surprise party with her family, and my family, and I'd love it if you, Sabrina and Jax were there too."

"Oh, we're there, but I thought you were waiting for her to be cool with the timing."

"Yeah, remember I told you that she surprised me with a gift?"

"Yeah. What was it?"

"A key to the condo."

"Her condo?"

"Yeah, with my name on the back of it."
This woman.

"Oh she's in-in!"

"Yeah."

"So you're probably ready for that double date Sabrina talked about then, huh?" he asked.

I was.

————

Just a week after Valentine's Day we met up with the two of them for some axe throwing and lunch. We weren't too serious about keeping score, but I had a feeling that I was probably going to end up in last place in every style of game we played. Dr. Chris was precise in everything she did, and I wouldn't count axe throwing as an exception. Sabrina was just competitive. So I figured between the two of them they'd be neck and neck for the top spot. Steve is good at everything, but he and I are pretty similar in how captivated we get by our partners. I once saw him almost bowl a 300. Sabrina showed up in the last two frames and this guy couldn't focus a lick. He tried to claim that he did it on purpose. But I think she drove him to distraction and now I knew the feeling.

I've had the chance to watch the love between Sabrina and Steve as it morphed through different stages of life, from dating, to marriage, to parenthood, to taking on the new responsibilities associated with caring for aging parents. They have held each other accountable and let things roll off their backs. They have held each other's heart through death and time's endless changes, and found their way back to each other like a boomerang after growing distant. That was the type of love I had always wanted to nurture with someone. Love that held on through storms and sunny weather. I hoped that Steve and Sabrina would shed a little light on some of the things we could to do help build a strong foundation for our relationship.

After Dr. Chris sufficiently smoked us in all of the games, the four of us sat down to chat over some good food.

"Steve, look at the way they're looking at each other over there," Sabrina said as she looked starry-eyed in our direction, one hand over her heart.

"Uh huh, I see 'em," Steve said.

I held Dr. Chris' hand under the table, like a kid who didn't want his teacher to see him holding his girlfriend's hand at lunch.

"I bet they're holding hands under the table right now," Steve said.

"Guilty," I nodded, drawing her hand up to my mouth for a kiss.

"We've been busted, Charlie," Dr. Chris chuckled.

"You don't have to stop on our account, now," Sabrina laughed. "Maybe that will rub off on us. We've grown so comfortable with each other that we don't do as much of the romantic stuff as we used to."

"Is that a bad thing?" I asked the two of them.

Steve responded before Sabrina, "I need to do better. I have the chance to love her forever, but I could do a better job of showing her how much I actually want to love her forever."

I had only thought about the two of them in how lovey-dovey they were in college. I never imagined that the spark would fizzle. It made me wonder if or when that would happen between Dr. Chris and I. I had watched my parents and grandparents actively love on each other in front of me, but I hadn't thought about what went on behind closed doors. I saw Dr. Chris nod at Sabrina's comment, but she hadn't moved after Steve's reply. I placed my hand on her knee so she knew I was with her.

Sabrina's body language became a bit more closed off before she spoke, shoulders slouched forward, lips pursed closely, eyes focused on the table in front of her, "I'd like that a lot Steve, it would help me know for certain that you still want me. But I need you to know that I'm still in love with you - even without it." He leaned over and kissed her on the cheek.

"When do you think things shifted?" Dr. Chris asked them.

"After year 3 of marriage for me,"

Sabrina said with sincerity.

Steve thought for a bit before speaking, "I think I stopped right around the time Jax was in her womb," he paused. "The thought of becoming a dad to me meant that I had to become the type of man my father was."

Sabrina interjected, "But he's his own man, Dr. Chris. I kept trying to tell him that he didn't have to parent or even live the way his parents did. You are your own man, your own person, you define who you are, babe." Sabrina said, directing her words straight to Steve. "You are the silly, strong, caring, warm, man that I met in college."

"The world tells me that I'm something different though. Or that I had to wear a mask to portray myself as something different. I just forgot I was wearing a mask and I started to take on its personality."

I knew the mask he talked about. It was heavy and cumbersome, but I was grateful that I could exist without it in the classroom and in the presence of Dr. Chris. "Did it feel like you lost yourself?" I asked him.

"Absolutely," he adamantly replied.

"How did you find your way back?" I asked, curious and in search of tools to add to my own arsenal.

"I'm still finding my way back, but-" he pointed to Sabrina. "This woman would not let me forget who I am. You saw how she just did that right?"

"Yeah," Dr. Chris and I said together, both observing from our own perspectives.

"She's always doing that for me, which is important for us. The world will try to ask you to dim your light so theirs can appear a little brighter."

I nodded, having experienced this in both corporate America and in the teacher's lounge.

"Don't you dare dim it," Sabrina said, looking at Dr. Chris and I. "And always hold each other up." The two of us nodded in concert.

"What's a part of marriage that you feel like most married couple's experience, but nobody told you about?" Dr. Chris asked them.

"Marriage is like a constant game of chess, except you're playing on the same team," Steve told her. "People always describe it as a need to compromise, and it is. Don't get me wrong!" he said leaning towards Sabrina. "We compromise on a regular basis, and I always appreciate her for doing it, because compromise is hard. BUT, we used to see it as compromising so the other person could win. Well, that means if someone wins, someone else is losing. But if we're supposed to be partners and I'm winning but she's losing, are we really partners? Now if we're on the same team and she compromises on taking the shot because I'm open, and the points I score with that shot happen to be the game wining points, did she lose? No! She got the win, and an assist."

"You just changed analogies, babe," Sabrina said.

"Fair enough," he said chuckling, "If I sacrifice my position as rook so she can get check mate, did I lose or did I help US win?"

"Either analogy he used is the truth, but I don't know how many married couples make it to that understanding. Same team man!" Sabrina laughed.

Dr. Chris and I looked at each other and nodded.

"So Charlie, I have a question for you," Sabrina said eying me suspiciously. "I think you're one of my favorite people, and obviously I love Dr. Chris by proxy." I nodded and squeezed her leg. "What are you going to add to her life?"

I was stuck for a moment, thinking about what on earth I could add to her life.

"I don't know that I know the answer to that, Sabrina," I was honest.

Dr. Chris asked if I'd mind her sharing what she thought I added to her life. I was kind of curious what her answer would be.

"You add a level of protection from the trauma associated with work and life in general. You add love at the highest level of surrender, which encourages me to love and live bigger."

"Well dadgum!!" Only Steve, could bring us out of such a heavy conversation with laughter.

"I didn't know you felt all of that, Chris," I shared, still stunned by her words.

"Charlie, what does she add to your life?"

"Sabrina, you gotta let that one simmer!" Steve joked.

"It's important for her to hear this, Steve. Trust me."

"So he needs to tell her that she's the glue that holds everything together for him, that he'd crumble under the weight of the pressure without her presence?"

"This is what he does, Dr. Chris," she said kissing her husband. "He's fast, but Charlie, that question was for you."

"She's," Sabrina pointed towards Dr. Chris, "You're my lighthouse, stoic in the distance, warning everyone where the shore is, keeping us all safe from the danger that we can't necessarily see, and ever present, allowing me to find my way back home."

It was the truth, but I hadn't expected tears to well in her eyes. Sabrina gave Steve a knowing nod and reached out to extend comfort through Chris' hand.

"I'll keep the lights on, Charlie," she joked.

I kissed her temple and held her close. *This woman.*

Just when I thought I couldn't possibly love her more, my friends stepped in and helped us see each other in an even stronger, brighter light. This was the exact conversation I needed to kick those birthday plans into high gear. I knew though, that there was one person I needed to speak with before contacting anyone else. I called her father the next day and asked if he'd be willing to meet me for lunch overmorrow.

———

We sat in a booth across from each other and caught up on how things were going with each other. I wasn't sure how to begin the conversation or what to do to segue into it, so I just jump stopped into a full pivot.

"Mr. James."

"Dad," he corrected.

"Dad," I nodded. "Thanks for meeting me here."

"Of course, Son. Is everything okay?" I think he sensed my nerves, so I acknowledged the elephant in the booth.

"Absolutely. I'm just a bit nervous because I've never had The Conversation with a man about his daughter before."

He sat back in the booth, his face stoic. "Take a deep breath and let it out, whatever's on your mind."

I did just what he'd asked me to do. I took one deep breath in, and upon my exhale I spoke from my heart, cutting straight to the chase. "Your daughter means the world to me and I want to ensure that I have your blessing to ask for her hand in marriage before I propose."

Still stoic, he responded with only one question. "Would you still love her if I said no?"

He's about to say no. I thought about it for a second and there was only one answer that was honest. Would it hurt? Yes. Would I be upset about it? Momentarily. But truth be told, "I think if you said no, then I'd love her enough to let her go. I wouldn't want to come between her and her family."

"I'd never do that to you, Charlie," he said, finally cracking a smile.

"Sir?"

"Chris, adores you. Because she loves you, I love you. And because you love her enough to put her needs ahead of your own desires, I trust that you'll continue to do that as you grow together. We're looking forward to welcoming you into the family, son."

A ten pound weight had been lifted from my shoulders. As we left lunch, I extended my hand for a shake, and he pulled me in for a hug.

"Thank you, sir."

I told him that I would be sending more details soon, but that I wanted to arrange a surprise party for her birthday - emphasis on surprise.

"Mums the word, Charlie."

"Thanks, Dad."

CHAPTER 9

BIRTHDAY PARTY EVE

Dr. Chris:

Iwas excited that we were about to spend the next 3 days together. Charlie called me as he was leaving school that Friday to let me know that he was on the way over. He had asked to spend the weekend at my condo so I didn't have to worry about packing a bag on my birthday. I told him that it didn't matter whose place we were at, as long as we had the chance to celebrate together. That's what mattered most to me. He was adamant about it though, so his call that he was on the way wasn't unusual. His reply to my question was though.

"Your text earlier today asked me to see if you grabbed your bag before you left, Charlie."

"Nnnnnnnope. I'm going to head to the house first to get my bag, and then I'll be headed your way. Are you interested in going out to grab some dinner tonight?"

Charlie had a strong memory. It wasn't like him to forget something like that. I had also told him that there was food on the stove, just waiting for him to get here. Apparently he forgot about that too because he asked me about going out for dinner.

"Charlie, there's food here that's already prepared."

"Dr. Chris, I forgot. There's just a lot on my mind that's all."

"Be safe, okay?"

"Roger that, ma'am. I love you."

I returned the sentiment and waited for his arrival. An hour passed and I was about to check in with him to see if he was okay when I received a text.

"Just leaving the house. Forgot to wrap your gift before I left this morning. Be there soon."

"Be safe, okay?"

"Roger. Love you."

"Love you."

About 15 minutes later, just as I was watering the honeysuckle bush that was growing near the window, I heard a key in my front door. In walked Charlie with a bouquet of flowers, a beautifully wrapped box, his duffle bag, and a smile that brightened up the entire space.

"Hey, Sugarplum," he said as he took off his shoes at the door. I loved the way he recognized me after we'd spent time apart. It was the same every time, and yet each moment felt unique in its own right.

I put the watering can down, and moved to the entryway to greet him. "Hi, sweetheart!" He patted my back during our hug instead of holding me the way he typically did. It didn't feel like home, and it didn't feel like Charlie. "Is everything okay,

Charlie?”

"Yeah, everything's good, Chris." He hadn't called me, Dr. Chris, in his typical flirty way. I didn't know what to make of it. Something was off. That nagging feeling in the pit of my stomach that something was wrong, just wouldn't go away. I didn't want to keep asking him about it, because he said he was okay even though he wasn't his typical self that night. But my ultimate goal was to let him know that I was here for him if he wanted to share.

Charlie:

Dr. Chris' birthday fell on a Sunday this year, and she had requested vacation at work, which meant we had all weekend to celebrate. We were supposed to start the party a little early as we were given a bonus day with this leap year. Trouble was, I had dueling responsibilities on that Friday evening.

This was the night that everyone was sneaking into town. I told them that I needed them to be at my house on time so I could let them in and head back to Chris' condo. But my family hit traffic on the way out of Arkansas. Steve wasn't answering the phone, which meant I had to stall so I could let them in, then I was extra late getting back to her place. I was so tired from teaching, and frustrated that my parents and grandparents were late that I wasn't in the best of moods when I arrived at Dr. Chris' condo. Her light helped me refocus on what was important for a split second. But that light was fleeting in this moment. I tried not to let it show, but I don't think I did a very good job of it.

She kept asking if I was okay. The truth was complicated. I was okay, but I was keeping a major secret from the person I was about to propose to. Everyone was going to be here to celebrate her tomorrow and she had no idea. While I was certain she was going to love it, there was still a lot of anxiety about whether or not our families would congeal. My parents had questions. Lots of them.

"What time are we supposed to be there tomorrow?"

"Is it here or is it at her condominium?"

"Do her parents know?"

"Are you going to do it before we get

there or do we get to see it?”
“Are you saving the hot dogs for tomorrow's party?”
“Where's your mustard?”

So many questions and they were texting them individually!

There we were trying to enjoy dinner together and my phone kept buzzing. I turned it face down so she wouldn't see who they were coming from. Eventually I turned the phone on Do Not Disturb so the vibrations of their texts wouldn't mess up the vibrations of our dinner. I excused myself to the bathroom and made sure I took my phone with me so I could reply to all of the emergencies.

“5pm at my house. They know. Haven't decided yet. Eat the hotdogs. Mustard is still gross - I don't have any.”

I assumed that would be enough to satiate them. I was wrong. As we washed the dishes together like normal, my phone rang. I knew it was one of my parents because the phone was on Do Not Disturb. The two of them, plus Dr. Chris were the only people whose calls could get through the DND filter. They had probably tried to text me while I was replying to everything. I slipped into her guest bedroom for some privacy as I answered the phone call.

"She doesn't know. You can't tell her. Just let me do it. I'll tell her when the time is right."

———

Dr. Chris:
His phone was going off non-stop at dinner. First he hid the screen from me, then he took it with him into the bathroom. Normally he'd just leave it on the table. But him taking it with him made me suspicious. That night was different. He already didn't seem like himself, then he was hiding his phone from me. He wouldn't really talk about his day during dinner and he wasn't his typically talkative self in general. When we were washing the dishes and his phone rang, he didn't answer it in the kitchen. He went into the guest bedroom, which was just on the other side of the wall from the sink.

I heard him trying to rush through the

conversation even though I didn't want to. I heard him telling someone that they couldn't tell me, to let him do it when the time was right because I didn't know. My thoughts were all over the place and my stress level was rising. Charlie had asked that I tell him if I ever felt like our relationship had the same uneasiness as the one I had with Trevor. In that situation, I could feel that something was off, but I told myself that things were okay. In this situation, I needed to see what was bothering Charlie. I knew that something wasn't right, and it didn't feel like there was another woman, but he certainly was off.

When he returned from the guest bedroom I had finished drying and putting away the dishes, and was sitting on the couch which seemed to annoy him.

"Charlie, what's wrong?"

Irritation filled his voice and his shoulders hovered up near his ears as he responded to my question. "Can't I just be? Is that okay? Can I just be still for a minute without being asked a question?"

I looked at him and took a breath before

opening my mouth to reply. I have a sharp tongue, and I knew I needed to temper my words before letting them fly out of my mouth like daggers.

"I know something's going on with you. I can tell it from your cadence around here to the way you just replied to me checking on your wellbeing. I don't know what it is and if you don't want to talk about it right now, no problem. But don't take out your frustrations on me."

He covered his eyes with the palm of his hand, his eyebrows scrunching up underneath them. Nodding he replied, "I'm sorry."

"I'm not going to ask again, but know that I'm here if you want to talk about it."

"It's been a really long day and I just want to veg out before we celebrate your day. I had big plans to prepare for this bonus day tomorrow and I didn't accomplish even half of them. I'm just a little stressed is all." Unhiding his face, he looked at me. I could see the sheer exhaustion on his face. "Forgive me?"

"Always, Charlie," I said as I leaned in to kiss his temple the way he usually kissed mine.

———

Charlie:
This woman. She was too good for me. Too understanding. Too openhearted. Too caring. Too considerate. Here I was lying to her face about what was going on, and trying to justify it in the name of my love and our future, and here she was loving me in spite of the crappy way I'd treated her, not because she didn't think she deserved any better, but because she knew me at my core, and she knew that the way I was acting was a reflection that something was internally off. And. She. Loved. Me. Anyway.

She'd turned on some cheesy movie about a couple in love and he was proposing in a big showy way in front of her friends and family. She made a comment that stopped me dead in my tracks, like a deer in headlights.

"He proposed in front of everyone?! 1) She seems like the kind of woman who would want something more intimate and private. I mean their whole relationship was intimate and private, and then he just proposes in front of everyone? 2) That's like the ultimate way to get her to say yes if she cares about you. Strong-arm her into not embarrassing you in front of all your loved ones."

Was I about to strong-arm her? My body locked up. My brain couldn't process what to do next. All I knew is there was no way I could propose tomorrow, not in the way I had planned. I had to rethink everything.

Marlo was due in town any minute and I knew he'd need help connecting with my parents so he could also stay at my place. He's the one who helped me pick out her ring. They had grown up together so he knew what she liked and what she didn't like. So here I was, with the ring of her dreams, and now no plan on how to propose. I was stressed.

I looked at my phone. I had missed 5 texts and 2 phone calls from Marlo. If I didn't call him back I knew he'd assume something was wrong and contact Dr. Chris. I excused myself again as soon as that dreadful movie finished, and found my way to the bathroom. I turned on the vent in hopes of muffling some of my conversation.

"Hey, sorry man. My phone was on Do Not Disturb."

"I lost your address and I need it for the ride share service."

I gave him the address and listened as he repeated it back to me incorrectly. The vent must have been interfering with our call. I hung up and texted him as fast as I could, but there was no reply. My message was stuck in the phone because the WiFi signal in the bathroom was nearly non-existent. I turned off the wifi in hopes of my phone connecting to the cell service. No dice.

I flushed the toilet and washed my hands so I could get back to a space where there was service before he got in a car that would take him to the wrong address. By the time I got back to the living room, I had received a message that my text was not delivered. I tried again and again, but nothing happened. I took my phone off Do Not Disturb and sat down on the couch only to realize that I actually needed to use the bathroom. So, just two minutes after I had returned from the bathroom I hopped up again and found my way back there. This time to actually use the facilities before returning back to the living room again.

About 20 minutes after we spoke, my phone rang again. It was Marlo, he was at the wrong house because he heard the wrong address. I apologized and explained to him that the reception was terrible in bathroom, gave him the correct address and then followed up with a text that actually went through this time.

I know Dr. Chris was confused. By all accounts I was acting squirrelly at best, and at the very worst, I was most definitely erratic and shady. She hung in there with me all night long as I hopped off the couch from the bedroom to the bathroom, to the kitchen to "get something to drink," to whatever excuse I could conjure up in an effort to give answers to those who had a seemingly endless list of questions.

When it was time for bed, I held her in my arms, glad that this stressful evening was over, but concerned that tomorrow would be less than I had hoped for. I couldn't help but feel that she knew I needed to be held myself. So she held me tightly. I could feel her love radiating from her soul. It took every ounce of strength I had to not weep in that moment. But I knew that she had me. My heart, had my soul.

———

Dr. Chris:

I heard him mumbling Marlo's name as he came out of the bathroom. It sounded like he was in town, but he hadn't contacted me. I figured Charlie was about to surprise me. The two of us had made plans to celebrate my birthday tomorrow instead of Sunday, and Marlo was unusually absent from my life. Usually I got a 1 month, 2 week, 1 week, and 1 day countdown to my birthday, but not this year. I hadn't received anything from him since the day before Valentine's Day. He had gone radio silent and I chalked it up to him having a Valentine that morphed into something more. Then I heard Charlie talking about him and disappearing into the bedroom and bathroom all night long. He was plotting something and Marlo was involved.

As we finished brushing our teeth and prepared to rest for the night, Charlie held me softly. It was a hug that I could only describe as one that felt like he needed me, like he needed help. So I turned in his direction and gave him all the love I had.

I let it ooze through every pore I had, hoping that at least one droplet of it would be absorbed by him. I could feel his heart pounding rapidly and listened as his breathing became shallow. His tense back muscles started to release themselves and he melded into me. I didn't move an inch. I just kept pouring love into his soul.

It seemed as though the more I poured, the more relaxed his muscles became. And the more relaxed his muscles, the stronger his breathing. Before I knew it, he had buried his face into my shoulder and I could feel on my skin, the warmth of the tears that flowed from his eyes and soaked into my shirt. I didn't ask any questions, I didn't speak a word. I just held on - giving him the best I knew how to give in that moment.

———

Charlie:
My heart, had my soul, and so I wept;
like a man who was overwhelmed with life,

like a man who was on the verge of losing his mind, like a man who needed his partner but didn't know how to say that. But she swooped in and gave me the very thing that I needed, without me even having to ask for it. I knew in that moment that I had been rushing the proposal, and I wanted it to be a private moment. There would be nothing private about tomorrow.

————

Dr. Chris:

I loved him through it, whatever it was. Then we went to bed.

CHAPTER 10
HAPPY BIRTHDAY

Happy Bonus Birthday, Beautiful," I whispered as she opened her eyes to the sight of me bringing her breakfast in bed. She sat up, wiping the sleep from her eyes, a smile beaming across her face.

"Thank you, Charlie! What time is it?" she asked.

"Don't you worry about time today," I said quietly, knowing her sensitive ears would be irritated if my words were filled with the amount of exuberance that was in my soul. "But it's 7:30," I finished.

She was giddy at the sight of the single light red carnation tucked within the lone purple hydrangea blossom. I admired and loved her beyond measure and I was hopeful that she would grant me the chance to get to know her on the deepest level possible - someday, but not today. Today was a chance for her to relax, relate, and release, though we were not going to tackle them in that order.

"Charlie, where's your breakfast?" she asked, always considering my experience as well.

"It's in the kitchen on the counter. I'll eat in there and come back and check on you," I said, pretending that I was actually going to do just that.

"You will not," she adamantly replied, her eyebrows furrowed in the middle of her face.

I stepped back, pretending to be aghast. "I won't?"

"I'll go get it for you so we can eat in bed together," she said quickly tossing the comforter off of her legs, almost draping the food on her tray with it.

"You will not," I laughed, serving her words right back to her on a silver bonus birthday platter. "I'll go get it."

She hollered down the hallway towards me as I left the room, "You better not eat in the kitchen!"

"I'm coming back woman," I told her, returning with a tray full of food. French toast, fresh cut fruit, bacon, and breakfast potatoes. All the same things that filled her tray.

We ate together, laughed together, and she shared with me the one thing she was most looking forward to in this year of life, "growing and learning, and hopefully traveling."

"It's on our list of promises for this year," I said, winking in her direction.

"Oh, the list of promises. Charlie, which one are we going to do this month?"

I shrugged, knowing that just on the horizon of the day we'd be checking off one more; host a small gathering together.

I cleared my throat, "We have time to decide that, but changing the subject back to today. You mentioned something about visiting a spa. Do you still want to do that?"

She sat pensive, clearly weighing her options. "Are we talking full facial and massage?"

"Whatever you want, Sugarplum. This is your day. I'm just the chauffeur," I said as her eyes filled with love and she danced in place while chewing one of her last bites of the French toast I'd prepared.

She took a sip of her favorite juice, clearing out any remaining food particles, then thanked me for breakfast.

I nodded, still waiting for her response to the Spa visit. She tapped her index finger on the bottom of her chin while looking up to the ceiling. "How about a couple's massage?" she finally replied.

"Oh girl, this is your day," I said.

"So was that a yes or are you about to sing, 'Only You', Slim?"

I smiled, I was busted in my attempt to sneak in some lyrics from her favorite 90s R&B group. I should've known better. She still asks her virtual home assistant to play their music on a regular basis.

"I'm not going to sing it, but if you want me to be there, with a towel draped across me, then I'll be there wearing the towel."

"What time are we going?" she asked as light danced in her eyes.

"There's a few options according to this app, but I'm guessing it might be best if we go early while their arms and hands are still fresh."

"Yep, probably so," she said.

"How does 10:30 work?"

"10:30 is great for me."

"Well let's get cleaned up. You hit the showers first and I'll bust some suds."

"I kind of like washing them together, Charlie."

"Are you telling me that you want to wash dishes on your bonus birthday?"

"No, I'm telling you that I want to wash dishes with you." She hit me right in the feels.

"Okay, well I'll go put water and soap in the sink, but I won't start washing them yet."

"And I'll hit the showers."

We got cleaned up and washed the dishes together, then took a moment to relax before the hustle and bustle of the day began. We made it to our couple's massage appointment with time to spare and in walked our masseurs. They talked us through the process and showed us where to change.

The two of us came out of the changing rooms in our robes and I couldn't help it. I whistled at my lady and smiled through the suppression of those thoughts, you know the ones. Let's just say I was looking forward to the day we got married. The massage artists, were skilled at their craft. I hadn't seen her this relaxed since New Year's day.

Our tables were right beside each other, as cliche as it sounds, I reached out for her hand as we were getting our massages. It was a transformative experience for me. I never thought I'd find myself on anyone's massage table, let alone on one being massaged by a man - we have such heavy hands. Yet here I was, with my bride, as my grandfather called her, laying on two tables, wearing the towel as she had requested after breakfast.

They finished the 45 minute massage and gave us 15 minutes to reset which included resting and getting dressed. We spent about 10 minutes of those laying on our respective tables, our fingers intertwined, sighing from achieving the ultimate level of relaxation.

She spoke slowly and methodically, "I don't want to move."

I lifted my head out of the face rest and looked around for the robes. "Uhh, Dr. Chris?"

"Yes, sweetheart?" she softly murmured.

"I think they took our robes away," I said seeking to inform and not incite a panic.

That didn't work out as planned though.

"What?!" she said quickly snapping her head up from the face rest on her own table.

We both looked frantically around the room. No robes in sight.

"There's some extra towels over there," I offered, knowing that I would be fine but that she, being a woman, had more body parts in need of covering.

"I guess I can use those," she said.

"Do you want me to go grab them for you or just put my head back down?"

"I can," she hesitated, seemingly flustered at the prospects in front of her, "I don't know!"

I tried to be reassuring, but part of me was tickled by the entire scenario. "I'm dropping my head down and closing my eyes. I'll just listen for the changing room door to close."

"You'll keep your head down?"

"Promise, beautiful," I said, my face already buried in the face rest.

"Okay, then I'm not going to grab the extra towels. I'm just going to grab the one I have and go."

"Okay," I said, closing my eyes and listening as her feet moved rapidly towards the changing rooms.

I heard her voice in the distance, "I'm in the room, Charlie," before the sound of the closing changing room door followed.

I sprang to my feet, slid into my sandals and hustled to the room to change. We only had a few minutes to spare before we were expected to exit, but we made it. The look on her face as we exited our changing rooms and made our way back to the lobby was priceless. Once we were back at the car, we laughed until my side hurt.

"I don't know why I assumed they would leave the robes there for us," I told her, wiping a tear from the outside of my eye.

"Next couple's massage is only coming

after we're married, mister!" she told me, while doing the same.

"Should we go get some lunch, Sugarplum?"

"Yes, let's get out of here!" she said, still laughing.

We went to our spot for lunch, The Fresh Pantry. We ate and laughed, and generally had a good time before we turned to story mode, generating fables and cautionary tales that aligned with our assumptions about the people walking down the street. We'd been at it for about an hour before the guy who changed my plans walked by.

"Ooh, that guy right there," she said, pointing to a Caucasian man wearing a fedora and sporting a navy blue blazer with a flower in the lapel.

"That guy? He's on his way to a date with a woman he met online. He definitely sees potential in her from their conversations thus far, which is why he's wearing the fedora that he picked up on his trip to Barcelona." She raised her eyebrows in appreciation of my creativity. "Your turn. The brown skinned woman with the natural hair, rocking the flower behind her ear."

"Plot twist. She's the date of our Caucasoid friend, which is why his Spanish fedora is so important. It's a sign that he's cool with everybody. She, however, is very proud of her culture, hence the twist out with the same type of flower that he had in his lapel. But her outfit," she hesitated, studying her ripped jeans, black t-shirt with the names of black female authors, and green camo jacket. "Her outfit," she began again, "says, I'm a writer with an appreciation of those who have come before me, but don't start a fight you can't finish. I'm not exactly reading date."

I nodded in agreement with her assessment until I saw another woman with the same flower walk by. "Uh oh," I told her, "I think our boy Fedora might be two timing the writer." We watched in silence as a fair complected woman in a dress sauntered by with a look of glee painted across her face.

"Surely not," Dr. Chris said.

I shrugged, hoping I was wrong. We finished up our lunch and headed out for the truck. I was driving so we were sitting up a bit higher than we would've been had we been in Dr. Chris' car. The extra height came in handy as we had a bird's eye view of the man in the Fedora striking out down the street, being chased by the two women sporting the same flower in their hair.

"Maybe you were right, Charlie."

I couldn't do anything except chuckle at the sight of our guy. "Dr. Chris, what if that happened to you?"

"What if it has already happened to me?"

"Has it?" I asked, concerned that her tone was hinting that she might have worn the same flower as another woman.

"It has," she finished straight-faced.

She proceeded to tell me about the first time she decided to meet up with a person she'd met online. I was mortified as she spoke about how he told her that he thought she wasn't going to show up so he invited another person to also meet him at the same time. You know, just in case, so he wouldn't look like he was stood up. I was livid by the end, but tried my hardest not to let it show.

"What did you do?" I asked her calmly.

"I walked out, blocked him, and said 'thank you' to God for not allowing me to go any further in building a relationship with that fool."

"Why would he think-" I paused.

"Why would he think what, Charlie?"

"Nevermind, I know why."

"Why what?" she asked with a look of worry.

"Why he would think you wouldn't show up."

"Why is that? I always wanted to know, but I definitely didn't want to ask him. You're actually the first person I've told about that."

"You are strikingly beautiful, and

intelligent, and caring, and funny, and he probably thought you were out of his league."

She blushed, "Charlie."

I shrugged again, "I just call it like I see it," I told her.

———

We drove around for a bit before finding our way to the park where there was a group of adults laughing in a circle. We watched them for a while attempting to figure out what was going on. One of them asked if we were here for the laugh therapy meet up. "Are we here for that, Dr. Chris?" I leaned in and asked her quietly, taking great care to move my lips as little as possible.

"Yes! Is this the right place?" she shouted in their direction.

"It is! Come and join us!" they laughed.

"Are we doing this?" I asked her.

"It's my bonus birthday, Charlie! We're doing this!" So jubilant.

So we laughed, in the park with strangers. At first it was awkward and I stood with my hands in my pockets, faking my laughter. But eventually, the laughter became real and my soul started to release some of the stress associated with the buzzing of my phone that I knew was tied to her next surprise. So we stayed in the park and laughed through the next 45 minutes before walking back towards Chief.

"That was actually a good stress release," I mistakenly told her as I reached down for her right hand, keeping my other hand in my pocket.

"What happened to the massage? How did your stress return?" she asked sounding doctorly.

"The thought of you being duped by that man brought the stress right back," I lied. "Can we swing by my house really quickly before dinner? I realized while we were out in the park, that I forgot to grab the right deodorant when I packed my bag last night," I lied again.

"Sure thing, Charlie. What's the plan after you grab your deodorant?" She leaned over and sniffed my armpit to assess how bad the need. I leaned away, hoping she wouldn't smell the Ocean Fresh scent being emitted, and instead writing her actions off as kind of weird.

"Wow. You must really love me, woman. You just sniffed my armpit," I laughed.

"I guess that is a little weird, huh?" she said leaning away, suddenly aware of how awkward that must have come across.

I squeezed her hand. "That's some stuff Sabrina and Steve do. My mom and dad, do it too," I said tilting my head down and raising an eyebrow in her direction.

Looking a bit blushed, she asked, "Are you calling it married people behavior?"

I nodded and asked as we arrived at Chief, "Have you ever sniffed a man's armpit before?"

"Not purposefully," she laughed in embarrassment as I opened the truck door.

"Just give me this one, Sugarplum," I said, helping her into the truck.

"I love you deeply, Charlie," she said as she waited for me to close the door.

"Are you in?" I asked, to which she responded only with a smile. I leaned in for a quick kiss before walking around to the other side of the truck. I opened the door to find her glancing in my direction, as if she were in search of a response.

"Oh! Right! I love you, Dr. Chris," I said with an ornery smile.

"What a fine way to treat your bride on her bonus birthday!" she said returning the smile.

I tilted my head towards the left, raised my eyebrows, dropped my mouth lower on my chin and harrumphed, "Hmm," before laughing and letting her know that I was only teasing. With that, I backed the truck out of the parking lot and headed towards my house. My phone buzzed and rang incessantly as we headed in that direction.

Dr. Chris asked if there was an emergency and I assured her that the most important person to me was sitting beside me.

"Just check, Charlie," she insisted. So I listened to the bonus birthday woman, and pulled into a parking lot so I could check my phone. There were messages from my parents and Steve, letting me know that everything was set up and that they had parked on Charlotte and walked to my house. I sent one group message replying that we were on the way and begging them to not send a reply that said okay. They didn't listen to the last part of that and my phone continued to buzz.

Dr. Chris asked if everything was okay and I told her that it was just my parents trying to wish her a happy birthday, not entirely a lie.

"Can I speak to them, Charlie?" she asked. I quickly glanced in her direction as I drove. Excitement was written all over her face. I couldn't very well tell her no. So I nodded and sent a quick text to the three of them.

"Parents, go up to my bedroom and close the door. Chris wants to talk to you. Steve, keep everyone else as quiet as possible. PLEASE."

My phone rang. It was my parents. It seemed almost too fast for them to really have gone to my room, but I answered it anyway - on speakerphone. I was really taking a gamble there.

"Hello?"

"Hi Charlie! Where's our birthday girl?" Mom asked.

"She's right here, Mom," I said passing the phone to Dr. Chris.

"Hi Mom!"

"Hi Chris! Happy Birthday to you, sweetheart," Mom gushed.

"Happy Birthday, Chris! We wish we could be there to celebrate you today," Dad replied, laying it on a bit thick.

"Thank you both! I wish you could be here as well, but Charlie has done a good job of spoiling me today," she told them as she winked at me from across the truck. I tried to keep my breath stable.

"Good! Hopefully, we'll be able to

celebrate soon," Mom said and I tried my hardest not to flinch. She was about to tip my hand so I spoke up.

"Soon, Mom! But hey, we have a dinner reservation that we have to make and we're cutting it close on time. I still need to swing by the house first to grab something before we change clothes and head to the restaurant. Can we call you back after dinner?"

"I mean, if you're not *BUSY* after dinner, you can call us back, Charlie," Dad said being a provocateur. I shook my head and Dr. Chris snickered while holding the phone as far away from her face as possible.

"Pop," I said, hoping to stop him from saying anything else borderline inappropriate.

"Charles, don't embarrass the boy," Mom uttered.

"Okay, so we'll call y'all tomorrow then?" I asked the two of them.

"See, I knew it Lois! I wasn't wrong. They're *CELEBRATING*, her

BIRTHDAY!"

I mouthed the words, "oh.my.God," in Dr. Chris' direction.

"Thank you both for the birthday wishes! We'll talk to you tomorrow okay?" she giggled.

"Okay, sweetheart! Happy Birthday! Enjoy dinner. Charlie, where are you taking her?"

"Mom, it's a surprise. If I tell you, then I ruin the surprise."

"I'm sorry. Okay, talk tomorrow. Be careful ton-i-i-i-i-ight."

I placed my face in my hands and mumbled between my palms, "Yes ma'am."

And with that, the phone call was done. I shook my head and without speaking a single word took my phone back from Dr. Chris before they could send a text to see how they did. I was right on time. No sooner than she handed it off to me did my phone buzz in my hands. I sent them a thumbs up then told Dr. Chris that Dad was apologizing for his out of pocket jokes. She rubbed my forearm which sent tingles down my spine. I winked at her and pulled out of the parking lot, headed towards the house.

There weren't any unusual cars parked in the driveway or in front of the house which meant that everyone had followed the plan accordingly. I put the truck in park and turned in her direction.

"Come inside with me?"

She eyed me with confusion, "You're just grabbing deodorant. I can wait in here."

I knew I needed to pull out the big guns to get her out of the truck, a little bit of begging.

I held her hand in mine, lifted it to lips and kissed her knuckles softly before giving her the puppy dog eyes and asking, "Pleeeeeeeeeeease, beautiful?"

Her shoulders climbed towards her ears, "Okay, Charlie."

I helped her out of the truck and we walked towards the house. I put my hands in my pockets, pretending like I needed to go back to the truck because I left my house key in the console.

"It's okay, Charlie. I have my key with me," she insisted. *Yes, I know you do.*

She turned the key, unlocking the biggest surprise I could probably have pulled off.

"Happy Birthday!!" they shouted in unison. She jumped and tossed her keys in the air. I caught them before they landed on her head and nudged her forward while she stared around the room in shock.

"Mom!!" she said pointing towards her mother. "Marlo?!" she asked, her hands cupping the sides of her face, confused at how he was in Kansas City instead of Colorado. "Vonne!! What are you-?" she said moving her hands to the top of her head and nearly choking on her words as she turned her head and saw my parents and grandparents. "Mr. and Mrs. Hughes!? I just spoke with you on the phone!!" She turned to me with tears in her eyes and rested a hand on my shoulder, "Oh Charlie!!"

"Happy Birthday, Beautiful!" I said

pulling her in for a hug and kissing her on the temple. "Go hug your family."

I stood near the door and watched as Dr. Chris moved from family to family, sharing time and space with them.

Her connection with her family, and mine was evident. Their connection to each other was heart-warming. Our parents had connected via video chat on Christmas Day, and we later found out that they had exchanged contact information and were regularly chatting with each other from afar. So when they met each other in person, they connected like old friends.

I watched like a spectator observing their favorite sport, and envisioned the day that this would happen with extended family at our wedding reception. One at a time, people came to me to ask if I had proposed yet or when I was going to do it that evening. One at a time, I had to explain to them with a smile that I couldn't pop the question until she and I were alone.

The truth is, I had hoped that our walk to the car from lunch would give me the chance to chat with her and possibly propose in the location of our first date. But that walk brought up "Fedora" and the similar situation she had once experienced.

With that out as an option, I drove to the park with the intent of finding a memorable spot for me to bare my soul and ask her to marry me. Then we stumbled upon the laughter meet up group and well, that was out.

So here I was instead, explaining to people that I couldn't do it yet. That the combination birthday/engagement party that I had promised them was only going to celebrate one. There I stood with my hands in my pockets, enjoying the sites and waiting patiently to make official what she and I have known since the snowstorm.

She was my person and I was hers for as long as she'd have me.

Chapter 11

The Morning After

Dr. Chris:

Itried spend the night at Charlie's house with his family, but his parents insisted we get in a little private time to end my bonus birthday night. So, Charlie drove us back to the condo with a promise for the 6 of us to meet for brunch on Sunday morning, my actual birthday.

We made it back pretty late that night and the two of us sprawled across the bed, laughing about how our parents seemed like they were becoming best friends. I told Charlie that I'd had a suspicion that Marlo was in town because of something he'd said the night before my bonus birthday, then asked if that's what had been bothering him.

"Yeah, I felt like I was lying to you all night and even into your birthday. You know how big I am on honesty, Chris."

I understood what he was saying, but this to me was different than someone lying to cover up their whereabouts or actions. I assured him that I knew his heart was in the right place. We held our post-celebration heart-to-heart until I was too sleepy to be coherent. That night, we fell asleep under the same cover. I just wanted to be close to the man who cared enough to send away for the very best.

There was only one lingering thing that I wondered, and that was why Charlie didn't propose. At some point during the celebration, every person who was there tried to slyly look at my ring finger, try being the operative word here. There wasn't one person who didn't do it. In fact, Grandpa Charles, held up my left hand and looked at me like something was wrong. I assumed Charlie had plans to propose but changed his mind. It was the latter part of that which slightly concerned me at the time, though I tried my hardest not to show it.

But having it take up residence in my mind was apparently too much. It soon became a thought that troubled me as I attempted to sleep through the night.

How do you shake off a nagging thought like that? You curl up beside the person who might be having doubts and see if they still hold you like they used to. At least that's what I did. I know it was irrational, but a tired mind gives way to absolutely the best-worst ideas in existence and that's where my mind went. I'm not saying it was right, but it happened.

So as I lay there beside Charlie, my head and heart prayed that he would hold me like he had when we slept on my couch through the snowstorm, and he did.

———

Charlie:

I cuddled with her through the night, grateful that she had enjoyed her bonus birthday, but concerned about how or when I would propose now. This plan had been in the works since February, but now things had shifted and I was faced with perhaps the most terrifyingly devoid of an answer question; now what?

My plan was busted and I didn't have a backup. I didn't know how to recover from that and I spent more time internally kicking myself while I was down, than I did focusing on how to pivot and determine what I could do to demonstrate my love for Dr. Chris. So I held on to her, savoring the tranquility that accompanied having her in my arms, before my brain would eventually turn towards chaos, churning on overdrive as it attempted to piece together another plan. Would my love carry me through the internal pandemonium? I certainly hoped so.

I awoke the next day, still holding her in my arms in the same position as we had rested the night before. I didn't know if it was fair to consider her my refuge, but she had unquestionably become my safe place. I wondered if that feeling was mutual as I looked at the calm that graced her face while she lay across my chest. Last night her worry brow was strong, but as she lay sleeping, there didn't appear to be a care in the world. I didn't want to wake her for fear of the return of her concern. I had a sense that her worries were something I instigated, but I didn't want to ask. The night had ended well and I didn't want to risk disrupting that. So I lay as still as possible, though one arm was numb from its hindered position. I loved her enough to let her sleep through my own discomfort.

I didn't know what would happen when she woke. I hadn't made plans for today. The only thing I knew for certain that needed to happen was brunch with my family. Mom had encouraged us to return to Dr. Chris' condo last night instead of staying at my house with them. I wondered if she had hoped that I would propose at the end of the day, giving them more reason to celebrate at brunch. I suddenly felt the urge to let them know ahead of time that I hadn't yet expressed my desire to grow old with her so there were no expectations going in. My phone was just out of reach though, so that message would have to wait.

———

Dr. Chris:
I could feel him moving while trying to stay still as I lay across his chest the morning after my surprise birthday

celebration. It was one of the most restful nights of sleep I'd had since Christmas Eve. There was something safe about his arms. I felt physically protected and my soul felt nourished by his. I never told him that though. It almost seemed unfair to put that type of pressure on someone. *'You're my safe place.'* I could imagine that making him more than a bit uncomfortable and possibly even adding pressure to always be the protector. It was just his innate desire to cover me that was shining through, and I didn't want any of that to become forced. So, I kept that information to myself.

I kept my eyes closed waiting for him to tap me, but he never did. I didn't know if he was still sleeping himself or half sleeping, or if he was waiting for me to move. I couldn't see him from where I was laying. I could only enjoy the cadence of his heartbeat and the rise and fall of his breath. When I felt him moving though, I knew he needed something. So I opened my eyes and caught a glimpse of him reaching for his phone, which was just beyond his grasp. I tapped out of his clasp and sat up in the bed, stretching my neck from side to side before leaning my weight back on my hands as they fell under the pillow behind me. Last night I had questioned whether or not he was second guessing his feelings about me. Gazing into his eyes that morning laid all those questions to rest. He still looked at me like he wondered how I found my way into his life. I'm sure I probably looked at him the same way as well.

"Good morning, sweetheart," I said smiling in his direction.

"Good morning, beautiful, Happy Birthday!" his morning voice rumbled. It was usually deep. In the mornings though, he could've pulled off an accurate cover of any Barry White song. This, hearing good morning from his lips, was one of my favorite parts of the day, whether that was in person or on the phone. It was a reminder of his love.

"Did you sleep okay?" I asked him as he shook his arm out.

"I did. Did you?" he asked through a toothy grin.

I nodded in return, thinking about the dream I had finished before waking up. I tend to have two types of dreams; fantasy based dreams where I know it's just a dream because of the tendency for inanimate objects to suddenly have personalities and take on human like behaviors. The other dreams are more prophetic in nature.

They're dreams that appear to be normal everyday occurrences with very specific conversations that stick to my memory like glue when I awake. They're definitely more realistic in nature and 99 times out of 100, I'll experience the dreamlike scenarios in real life, exactly as they played out in my dream. The dream I had that night, or morning if you want to get specific, was definitely one of the latter. I didn't know how it was possible that it would happen, but I trusted that I'd see it come to fruition at some point. I just had to find the patience within me to wait it out. That would be the real challenge.

I didn't realize in my daydream state that Charlie had been trying to ask me a question. Suddenly I snapped back to reality after hearing his laughter.

"I'm sorry, Charlie. What did you say?" I asked feeling embarrassed about getting caught slipping.

"You kept nodding and staring at me so I asked if you needed anything," he said.

Still sheepish, I replied, "My bad. I'm good. Thank you."

He continued to chuckle. "You sure? It looked like you wanted something."

"Oh, you have no idea," I said rising from the bed and entering into a full body stretch and shaking my head. "You have no idea," I repeated, thinking again about that dream and what I wanted."

He smirked at me, I'm sure his mind was fixated on something else, but I knew in my core what I wanted.

Charlie:
She looked at me like she was holding in her deepest desire. I only hoped that I would have the opportunity to help fulfill whatever that was. I looked at my phone after she started stretching, remembering that I needed to text my parents an update. So I sent them a quick message.

"Morning y'all. No additional updates from last night. Brunch as normal today, please."

"Oh Charlie, what are you waiting for?" Mom replied immediately.

"The right moment, Mom," I fired back.

"In your time, Charlie. Just make sure she knows you love her every day," Dad replied.

———

The two of us met my family to eat at one of the most widely known brunch spots in Kansas City. Together we ate and laughed about the party and Dad asked about Marlo and his Valentine.

"Now how many years have they been dating?" he asked.

"To our knowledge they just started, but knowing Marlo it's possible that he looked for a job in Colorado because they'd been secretly dating for a while," Dr. Chris replied. That actually made a lot of sense to me because of the conversations I'd had with him, which of course, I couldn't tell Dr. Chris about yet.

"What made you ask that, Dad?" I asked him.

"They just had a natural tempo about them," he said, glancing back and forth between the two of us like he was trying to decide if he should say what was on his mind. This was my dad we were talking about. I knew the only way he wouldn't say it was if Mom stopped him. "It was almost as natural as the two of you," he said with a shrug.

Dr. Chris leaned into my arm and rested her head on my shoulder. I rubbed my cheek up against the top of her head, catching a whiff of the moisturizer she used to keep her coils supple. I hadn't even realized that I moved until mom made a noise.

It was akin to a whimper, but more jubilant in sound. Dad patted her on the arm as if to comfort her and let her know that it would be happening soon enough. My grandparents grinned over at the two of us. I smiled at the whole scene. My "bride" and I, brunching with my family.

My heart was so full. I wanted to ask her in that moment. I wanted to drop to my knee and officially give her the heart that she already had. Before I could do it, she asked my family if they'd mind her taking the video chat request that was coming in to her phone.

"Hey Marlo!" she smiled. "I'm at brunch with my family," she said turning the phone so Marlo could see which family she was referring to.

"Hey Family!" Marlo waved.

They chatted only for a short while before he invited his Valentine to join him, flashing her engagement ring for Chris to celebrate. She was genuinely excited for the two of them, but I could see a hint of "thought it'd be me" in her shoulders, which was just out of eyesight of the phone's camera. Marlo was unable to see it, but my grandparents, parents and I all caught it. I looked at them for help and they nodded in my direction that it would all be okay.

"Remember my text," Dad mouthed in my direction. I nodded then quickly smiled when she looked in my direction after getting off the phone with Marlo.

"Thank you for sharing that moment with me. I didn't know they were getting engaged," she said.

"It's quite alright sweetheart," Mom told her.

My grandparents hugged the two of us as they prepared to get on the road headed back to Arkansas, and Dad and I helped them into his truck. Mom gave me a light hug and I thanked her for joining us this weekend before turning to say goodbye to my father. As I man-hugged Dad, I turned in time to catch a glimpse of Dr. Chris and my mom, squeezing life into each other. I loved how they loved each other.

"We'll see the two of you soon, okay?!" she said fighting back tears.

"Call us when you get home, Mom," Dr. Chris replied.

I wrapped my left arm around her lower back, keeping my right hand in my pocket. They waved as they were leaving the parking lot in Dad's pickup truck and I focused my attention to Dr. Chris, who was fighting through tears of her own.

"Hey! You okay, Sugarplum?" I asked her through a kiss on her temple.

She nodded, and told me she wished they could have stayed longer or that we could've spent more time with them while they were here.

I apologized, still feeling guilty about keeping them from her. "Next time we'll do that, okay?" I asked. She nodded.

"I still can't believe Marlo is engaged!" she said, shifting the conversation.

"I mean, they looked pretty comfortable with each other," I said, not realizing that I was digging my own grave.

"They did, but I mean, aren't we comfortable with each other too, Charlie?" she asked, as if to clarify whether or not I was saying Marlo and his Valentine were more compatible than the two of us.

"We're very comfortable with each

other, and compatible too I think," I said, wondering if this was the right time to propose. Would we have to call Mom and Dad back to the restaurant? Would it look like I only proposed because Marlo had selfishly gotten engaged? I knew it wasn't selfish. I was supposed to have proposed already. I was just mad that I hadn't stuck to my guns and now I was mulling over whether or not she'd question the motive behind my own proposal. I did it to myself.

Dr. Chris:

He just stood there, hands in his pocket, fiddling about like something was bothering him.

"Where to sweetheart?" I asked, hoping to break his trance. His head snapped in my direction, eyes locked with mine, as he tried to hide his shamefaced smile.

"Wherever you want, ma'am. I got time today," It almost felt like a sense of foreboding followed immediately behind his sentence. I tried to shake it, but it followed us around the rest of the day. It was there as we went to catch a matinée. It was there as we found our way to get jumbo pretzels. It was there as we sat at my favorite spot at the lake.

I tried to enjoy the time we were spending together, but there was an overbearing sense of impending doom that was on its way. Try as I might, I was unable to shake it.

CHAPTER 12

DAYLIGHT SAVINGS TIME

Dr. Chris:

The foreboding that I felt the day after my bonus birthday celebration, followed us through the week, all the way to the following weekend. He had time on that day for the two of us to spend together, but we'd barely seen each other all week. Between his schedule and mine, time was a commodity we had forgotten to budget for.

Monday: Charlie's regular schedule was extended as they prepared for their students to take assessments. He had meetings before and after the school day and was understandably exhausted by the time the evening had come. We spoke after my shift and again before bed, but we didn't see each other on that day.

Tuesday: Charlie was tasked with leading his grade level on the assessment prep for English Language Arts, a major accomplishment. I brought dinner to his place to celebrate. He was so exhausted, he fell asleep at the table. I helped him to bed and returned to my place for the night, leaving a note for him to find in the morning.

"Wanted you to rest. Dishes are done. Love you, deeply."

Wednesday: I awoke to a text from Charlie, thanking me for dinner and taking care of him and the dishes. He also apologized for falling asleep on me. I told him in my reply that it was my pleasure to take care of him and that no apology was needed. He asked if I'd be able to visit him that evening, and I reminded him that I was scheduled for a double shift. That evening he sent dinner to the hospital with a note.

"I love you deeply, and I got the dishes."

Thursday: I gave him the choice between a late night or an early morning phone call. Neither of them were 100% good for either of us, but he opted for the late night call in his words, "to make sure I could stay awake on the job." I told him there was coffee. He showed up to the hospital early that morning as my shift ended, to walk me to my car and ensure I made it safely back to the condo to rest. He tucked me in and kissed me good night, before leaving me a note and heading off to teach for the day.

"My turn to take care of you. Breakfast or lunch - what time is it now? - is in the fridge. Love you, deeply."

I sent him a text after I woke up. It was 11:30 in the morning. "Thank you for last night, and for brunch! Love you."

Friday: I had the day off, and Charlie picked me up straight after he was finished teaching so we could spend the evening together. I had to work Saturday, but I was off on Sunday. Friday we were both so tired that we fell asleep on the couch trying to binge watch a series that made zero sense on paper, but was more intriguing than I would have envisioned when I read its description.

Saturday: I worked, while he was off. But Jessica somehow found an excuse to spend time with him. She rushed out of the house when I came home, which caught Charlie off-guard. I sure didn't get a good vibe from her and that was something I had learned to trust instinctively. When I was younger and things were off, I usually felt a nagging sensation in my gut before things were revealed.

I had felt the nagging sensation with her when she returned Charlie's phone to him before MLK day. It was there again when I had the opportunity to connect with her about the Valentine's Day planning that she and Charlie did "for the kids." She was manipulative at best, and her reassurance that she was just there "to help" felt contrived at the worst. Though it took some effort initially, I tried to pay attention to the thoughts I was feeding, and focused my effort on spending time with Charlie instead of combating Jessica. She was showing herself and at some point, I assumed that Charlie would see it for what it was. Nevertheless, her actions were still irritating.

I watched her look back towards his house like she was waiting for him to say goodbye. *Nope, it's just me ma'am.* Charlie was too preoccupied with grabbing my bag and preparing a fresh juice to welcome me home to see her goal of running interference. I wanted to ask him about it. I also wanted to protect my peace. So I just let it go.

Sunday: We only had 23 hours to spend together, which I know sounds like a lot. But when you've barely seen or spoken with each other all week, you want the full 24 hours promised in a day. But on that day, Daylight Saving's time took effect. We sprang forward and Charlie wanted to commemorate it with a special "spring" themed date.

He started with a trip for the two of us to volunteer at the food kitchen as we promised we'd do together monthly. He and I served breakfast to those who were interested and chatted with them about their life stories. There were military veterans who had fallen on hard times after service, there were families who weren't able to recover from the effects of the 2008 recession, and generally speaking, lots of people who were tootling along through life without knowing that things were about to take such a drastic turn for them. Theirs were the stories you saw in movies, except they were living through the trials and hadn't yet reached triumph. Charlie and I had the chance to chat about the stories we'd heard over our lunch in the park. Hearing how he related to the core of their experiences further solidified my faith in him as a human being. My love grew deeper still.

Before we left the house, he had packed up the car, including a blanket and a basket, but it wasn't uncommon for him to pack extra gear just in case we might possibly need something while we were out. Ninety percent of the time we never used the stuff he packed, which worked out in his favor today because I hadn't suspected a thing. He rolled out the blanket on the museum lawn; its grass in the process of shifting from dormant to active growth. The sunlight looked like jewels shimmering in through the branches of the trees, which were showing the promise of buds. We had a view of the tulips and the city in motion. The beautiful scenery was a bonus. I didn't need much, just Charlie and food, and I was good.

———

The time we were shorted on Daylight Savings Day, was indicative of the amount of time that the two of us would get to spend together in the coming weeks. He and I first fought to find time to connect. Then we struggled to find time to connect, both in person and via phone. As much as I loved him, this was taking a toll on me. Every conversation we had centered on his students and Jessica.

Eventually I started to tune him out. I tried my hardest to listen, but it was hard to hear him talk about someone who got to spend more quality time with him than I did. I never considered myself the jealous type, and yet there we were.

I waited until we had the chance to connect over a weekend lunch, finally taking a deep breath and telling him how I was feeling. It was one of the hardest things for me to admit. Let's all be honest. Nobody wants to be the jealous partner in a relationship. Insecurity, fear, rejection, anxiety. I didn't want to embody any of those feelings, but not talking about it early had led me through the first two. So I decided to tell him where I was coming from, before we found out what the rest looked like on me.

There we sat, me with my hands in my lap underneath the table, feeling the words as they started to bubble to the surface, and Charlie, smiling away, not knowing what was about to hit him.

"Charlie, I never thought," I paused to clear my throat and start again, "I'm not sure where to start with this conversation, so I'm just going to jump in right in the middle and fill in the blanks where I can. I know you're going to have questions. Feel free to ask away," he looked instantly concerned.

There was a hint of worry in his words, "Okay?"

"I love you deeply, but I realized over the course of the last few weeks that I'm battling a fear that you have no control over," I started.

"What is it?" he asked, reaching out across the table for my hands.

I placed mine in his and continued, "It's the same fear that I held when we first started dating. Remember when I told you that I was trying my best?"

He nodded, "You were on the couch after Oakley called in the middle of the night."

"Yep, that's the time." He continued nodding and listened as I spoke.

"I was looking for the words to express it then. And I feel like I kind of did, but not to the extent that I was hoping I'd be able to express myself."

"Do you want to try again?" he asked while caressing the tops of my knuckles - his go to soothing technique.

It was my turn to nod, "I do."

"I'm listening," he said as I opened my mouth to try and explain it again.

"I was totally caught off guard by your love. I didn't see it coming. But I embraced it once it found me. I need you to know that I truly love you deeply."

"I know you do," his worry lines started to crease his forehead.

"I'm battling through the fear that this will end up the same way that my last relationship ended. I know you're not Trevor. You don't show any of the same characteristics, and basically everything is 1000 times better than that relationship ever could have been even if it wasn't dysfunctional. But there's a fear that lingers, a fear that I'll be left again."

In his urgency to let me know that he didn't have any plans to do such a thing, he cut me off as I was still speaking, catching himself before he went any further, "I'd never-"

"I know you say that, Charlie. But it's MY fear that I'm battling. That doesn't have anything to do with you or your actions. It's MY brain that I'm in a battle with. But, I'm working really hard to do better, which is why I need to tell you what I'm feeling right now."

His breathing was so shallow I was concerned that he had unconsciously stopped, "What is it, Chris?"

"I'm big jealous right now that Jessica gets to spend so much time with you, and I'm struggling to find time. I know you want to spend more time with me, and that this is a short term problem, but that's my battle right now."

He nodded before speaking, "So it probably doesn't help your jealousy when I'm here talking about all the ways she irritated me at work, does it?" I shook my head in reply. "-because at the end of it all, she was still spending time with me where you wanted to," I nodded and so did he.

"I know it's not something you can control, Charlie, but I need you to know that my inner dialogue is in a battle with itself and I'm hoping that this conversation will help the correct side come out victorious," I joked.

He squeezed my hand, and gazed intently at me. The smile faded from my face. "Thank you for trusting me enough to tell me that," he said sincerely.

And just as fast as that smile had disappeared, it quickly returned.

Charlie:

I knew that something had been bothering her. There were times when she was fully present, and times when she would emotionally check out. I mean, all the way out. Like, I'm inserting random facts about cartoon characters from the 90s into our conversations and she would "mm hmm" like that had something to do with what we had been talking about before.

So it was good to learn where the challenge was and it helped me to be more mindful of sharing the frustrations I'd encountered with Jessica during my conversations with Dr. Chris. I stopped accepting her requests to stop by to help with the prep work for Assessment Week, and instead just worked on it myself. Her actions weren't anything new, as she and I had collaborated on a lot of responsibilities throughout the first semester of school, but I didn't have a lady in my life at the time. It hadn't crossed my mind how it might feel to Dr. Chris, until she said something.

To be honest, I was a bit fearful myself as she began to speak. It felt like she was about to end things and I was trying to figure out where it was coming from. My own anxiety started to rear its ugly head and I knew for certain that I needed to listen well and listen hard because I still had something that I hadn't yet asked her. I was hoping that Daylight Savings Time would be the day to do it, but that didn't happen.

Then I thought I'd pick a random day when the feeling struck me, but we just hadn't spent that much time together. I felt like I was running out of time, to be honest. So when she started speaking, really telling me where she was struggling, it felt like she was about to say something that would end things for us and my heart started to ache. I think I held my breath for a moment. I'd known since day one that she was my wife, but I hadn't told her everything that was on my heart, and I thought it would end up costing me the woman I loved.

Dad had asked me to show her every day that I loved her and I admit, I fell short on that the last few weeks. I falsely assumed that my complacency within our relationship was about to do me in. Then she shared the thing I had hoped to hear since the night we picked out Randolph, that which she feared the most. Her greatest fear wasn't an animal or death, it was something much more human, a fear I actually shared with her; a fear that we'd lose something and someone who meant to world to us.

I couldn't speak for her, but I could speak for myself. That fear had so much power because I was concerned about what was on the other side of that loss. For me, it was a fear that I'd lose the person who meant the most to me in the world and that I'd be a crumbly mess on the other side of it, that life wouldn't hold as much meaning on the other side of it, that I'd end up a cantankerous old man on the other side of it because truth be told, if I lost her, if I lost Dr. Chris, I wouldn't be as kind to the world around me. The world to me would lose a lot of its light.

Yes, I realized that was a lot of power to give to someone. But I held her in that high a regard. There wasn't a thing that could have been said to change my mind because of who she was and who I was when I was with her. I was different. Life was different, and I didn't want to return to the semblance of life that I was living before I met her.

First semester and second semester were two totally different time periods for students, and the same was holding true for me as well. I was growing and I knew that Old Charlie was a thing of the past. I couldn't go back without feeling like I had failed at life.

"Thank you for trusting me enough to tell me that," I said. My body was overflowing with emotion and I was ready to tell her about my heart. I wanted her to know that I was ready to love her forever. I sat back in my chair, placed my hands in my pockets and steadied myself to stand beside her.

"Thank you for listening," she said before rising to her feet. "I'm going to head to the ladies room before we get out of here." I nodded, knowing that my already narrow window had just closed.

I was going to find a way to ask her. I was going to find the right time, and there wouldn't be any distractions associated with that time. I kept telling myself that I'd know instinctively when it would be time. But the truth was that I was pushing my luck. She was right that we hadn't spent much time together. One might even say that we were starting to drift. My heart wasn't drifting, but I needed to do a better job of making room for her as a priority. I was looking forward to Spring Break so she and I could reconnect and we could discuss the future. More specifically, so we could discuss our future.

———

Spring break came and went, and although I wasn't at work, we still didn't get to spend much time together. I hoped that I could deliver lunch, but with students being out of school, that meant her schedule became more packed during the day. Because her schedule was more packed during the day, that meant that she was worn out by nightfall. Because she was worn out come nightfall, I found myself preparing meals for her and washing dishes by myself even though she wanted to help me. I stepped in to help her in the same way she'd helped me when I was overwhelmed with assessment prep. We were a team, but I still didn't have the chance to reconnect with each other the way I had hoped to.

That week gave me the opportunity to

show her how much I loved her everyday, but I wouldn't propose to her when she was barely coherent. That just didn't seem right to me. I could have tucked her into bed and bared my soul to her but she likely would have fallen asleep in the middle of my monologue. I could have tried to wake her earlier than normal, but she likely would have rolled over and gone back to sleep. There was no ideal time to do it anymore and I had almost resigned myself to the idea that I was just going to have to blurt it out some day when I was so moved.

Would that be romantic? No. Would it get the job done? Yes. Did she deserve the best? Absolutely. Was blurting it out the best? Not even remotely close. So I was back to devising a plan. I just needed some time to figure out the move. The problem was, the time I needed was pushing us further and further apart. She was tired. I was tired. We had little spats here and there, but nothing abnormal. By the time April arrived, the spats had become our norm. We were teasing each other and communicating like an old married couple, except I hadn't yet asked her to marry me, which would prove to be a problem.

CHAPTER 13
EASTER TRIAL

Charlie:

By the time Easter arrived, our relationship had become fully engulfed in flames. I definitely wouldn't have predicted this given the way the tide turned in our favor on Christmas Eve. But regardless of what I had anticipated, it didn't change the outcome.

Things had moved swiftly between Dr. Chris and I. This was supposed to be different. She was supposed to be different. My heart was supposed to be different. Maybe we rushed things. Maybe in our excitement, we moved too fast and what we thought we felt as love was actually just infatuation.

There we were in the middle of our

worst disagreement yet. I had accused her of not trusting me, my second greatest fear realized. She had accused me of failing to hear what she was actually saying, which in hindsight was probably true. While we hadn't raised our voices at each other, things were definitely heated and tense, and I didn't know how to find my way back. Apologizing wouldn't take away what I'd said. It couldn't take back the fact that I had failed to fulfill my promise to take care of the heart walking outside of my body. I had treated her like she was disposable because I didn't like the truth she was seemingly shoving in my direction. I felt like I was on trial.

It was too much. It overwhelmed me. I felt like I was incapable of loving her. So I reverted back to Old Charlie, and acted in haste. I didn't think through anything and I pushed her away, just before we were supposed to go to her parents' house for Easter Dinner.

———

We had attended Church that morning and fellowshipped with many of our friends and colleagues. After service was over, we were headed towards Chief when we noticed that Jessica was waiting for us.

"Lord be with me," I said aloud. She had become more emboldened the more distance I put between us.

"Hi Charlie!" she shouted, hugging me far too long for it to be Christianly. I tried to wriggle away, but she was far stronger than I had known to be true. I held onto Dr. Chris' hand hoping she would save me. I'd later find out that she had expected me to say something.

"Jessica," I said very formally and standing straight as a board trying my best not to move, lest she think it meant something it did not.

"Happy Easter, Charlie," she said completely ignoring Dr. Chris even though I was still holding onto her hand for dear life.

Dr. Chris cleared her throat. There was dread tied to that moment. I can hear it right now thinking about it again. It was one of those moments in which I knew things could not go back to where they were before the moment existed. We couldn't pivot around it. There was an entirely new stake in the ground.

Just the night before she had asked me about whether or not I still saw her as my bride. It had caught me off guard and I didn't know how to move forward from there. I stammered through my answer, trying my hardest to figure out how to tell her that I didn't want anyone else but her. I wanted with all my might to let her know that she was the only person in the world who could make me feel all 27 human emotions, many of them simultaneously. Instead what came out was, "Uhh, what do you mean do I still consider you to be my bride? Umm, why wouldn't I still feel like that? Ahh, how could you even ask me that question?"

What I should have said was simple. One word. Yes. Instead, I was standing there looking like I had something to hide. I know she could feel it. I couldn't take it back. I had just become the same guy that I warned my cousins about when we were growing up. So couple last night, with me not speaking up and presenting Dr. Chris to Jessica while she waited for me out of the blue, and you had yourself a hotbed that was ready to flare up at any moment.

Laying across the coals was our relationship and I had placed it there. I had dropped it on the skewer last night and then laid the skewer on the spit after church. The flames of fear licked the sides of the skewer and my fraudulent indifference set it all ablaze.

I'd had to pull the truck over so the two of us could talk because things were so heated and confusing I could hardly pay attention to the road. I wasn't willing to sacrifice her safety or mine for the sake of making a point, so we drove to the same park where we overlooked the city at the turn of the New Year.

She spoke softly, "Am I standing in your way, Charlie?" I wondered if she feared my answer.

"Why would you even ask me that?" I asked. My answer should have been simple. One word. No.

She unloaded her thoughts on me. "Because it feels like you've been drifting away from me recently. When I ask questions about your day, you shoo me away or don't share much information anymore. When I take interest in what you're doing, you act like my questions to learn more are questions meant to keep you from doing whatever it is that you're interested in doing. It's maddening. We haven't spent much time together at all and when I ask questions to connect with you, I get met with resistance or this sentiment that I'm somehow trying to stand in the way of you doing something, in spite of my insistence that I'm trying to stay connected to you. Am I standing in your way?"

I didn't have any words. I felt attacked by hers. She had held up a mirror and I didn't like what I was seeing, so I told her she was wrong. I fed her excuse after excuse to justify what I actually owed her an apology for doing. She was seeing the worst of me in this moment and she chose her words carefully to figure out if she was still of value in my life. We were trapped in the truck. It felt like the walls were closing in on me.

"Charlie??" she was clearly waiting for me to answer the question instead of dodging it by asking her a question in return.

I sat in silence, staring at her. Mad at the world because she was holding me accountable for my crap. Mad at myself because I could see the hurt in her eyes - caused by my bogus impassiveness. That new stake that was planted in the ground gave us the chance to move forward or backwards, but we couldn't stand still anymore. I was now pivoting around our actual future and not just the idea of it.

I placed my hands in my pockets, running my fingers over the box that had been a daily staple in my wardrobe since the night before her bonus birthday, and refused to speak. I didn't want to say anything else that would risk it. I knew what I wanted for us but I had done a terrible job of communicating that to her. So, as I sat still, so as not to say something else stupid that I couldn't take back, I didn't realize I was sending her a crystal clear message.

My answer should have been simple. One word. No. Instead it came across as me not wanting to tell her that she was standing in my way. She sat still, tears filling her eyes as she mourned the loss of our relationship at the very same time that I was trying to figure out how to propose to her. The juxtaposition was absurd.

It burned in effigy. You hear people say that all the time to describe physical buildings that are representative of something disliked as they go up in flames. But this was true of our relationship. It felt as though the one on fire above the coals had been a mockery of the relationship we actually thought we were in. I watched it go up in smoke, unable to speak, unable to move, unable to assess whether or not it was really happening until she quietly removed her house key from her keyring and placed in the cup holder between us. It felt like a punch to the gut, but I sat as stoically as I could to keep my emotions in check.

"I'm not going to stand in your way anymore. I'm also not going to beg you to see me, to love me. I love you deeply, Charlie," she said as the tears painted her cheek a darker shade of brown.

I stared at the key in disbelief. How did we get here? I couldn't envision my life without her, in spite of this argument, but she didn't want to be with me. Pride was an ugly thing, and mine got in the way of everything in that moment.

I could have told her what I really felt. I should have made it clear last night and after church, and when the disagreement started, but at every single turn, I was too arrogant, too hubristic to tell her the truth. As I sat in my own truck, staring in disbelief at the house key that my bride had just returned to me, I felt like an incompetent man, unable to love her the way she needed. I knew that she deserved better. I knew there was nothing I could do or say in that moment that would change what I had just communicated to her, so I picked up the key, stuffed it in my right pocket and shook my head, internally distraught with emotions that I wouldn't allow to rise to the surface. I wanted to scream. I wanted to punch the air. I wanted to wail. Instead I sighed, afraid to move and afraid to love. This one hurt me as deeply as I loved her.

"Where do we go from here?" I nearly whispered to her.

"I'm going to need some space, Charlie."

I reached for her hand which I was hoping she'd allow me to hold just one last time. I was grateful that she did. I hoped she could feel the warmth that was ever present between us and remember that I loved her. I hoped she could see the anguish I was in as I was about to hyperventilate trying to hold in a ball of entangled emotions. I knew though that hope was a muscle you had to flex. So I told her the truth.

"I love you deeply, Chris. I always have. I always will."

She removed her hand from mine to hold her head and weep within them. I prayed that He would get us through this trial together before realizing that what I wanted might not have been His will. So I prayed for that instead and released it into the Universe before driving us back to her condo per her request.

I wanted to fight for her, but I didn't think it would be well received. So, I let go.

I let go of my dreams. I let go of my expectations. I let go of us. I let go of my heart.

———

Dr. Chris:
I didn't understand how he could just let

go, how he couldn't fight, how he wouldn't give us a chance of survival. My heart ached something serious, but there was no way on earth I was going to ask for someone to love me. I hoped he would step up. I hoped he would be the human I knew him to be. I hoped he would give himself the same grace I was willing to extend. I hoped he would tell me what he was thinking. But he couldn't get out of his own way enough to see me, to see us, and so I let go.

I let go of the dream I had the morning after my birthday surprise. I let go of the vision I had of our family. I let go of us. I let go of home.

CHAPTER 14

THE AIR OF SPRING

Charlie:

I walked into my house after dropping off Dr. Chris, and thought about all the times she referenced this as home. I had missed it before. "I'm on my way home, Charlie," she would say when she called after her shift.

When we were supposed to meet at her place it was always, "I'm on my way to the condo, Charlie." That wasn't her home. This was her home, and she wasn't in it. The first night I was in shock. I sat in solitude hoping it had been some sugar induced dream that I'd awaken from at any moment. The problem was that I was awake. I had been awake since we fixed breakfast together before church, and I would be awake until the sun rose the next morning.

I was no good at school the next day, completely numb and going through the motions. The principal called in a sub when she saw me, sending me home immediately. Jessica tried to insert herself into my business as I was trying to leave before any students arrived. She had five million questions and I had nothing to say to her because I knew any small amount of information, even just six words, would be turned into a ten page essay for her unrequested all staff report. I just wanted to rest. So I brushed by her, not even looking in her direction, not giving her any attention at all, and left through the school's side entrance on my way to Chief. I sat in my truck, exhausted by the weight of the world and finally cried. I cried as I put on my seat belt, and as I started the ignition, and as I put the truck in drive and left the school grounds. I was not okay.

My chest was tight and my back ached. I was having trouble breathing through the tears. I was a wounded man, and I just wanted to get back to my house to lay down. I was just around the corner from the house when I noticed a police car tailing me through the neighborhood. I prayed that he be on his way elsewhere when I saw him flip on his lights and heard the siren blare.

Here I was, an emotional and exhausted human being in need of compassion, and I had to pull it together enough to pull to the side of the road and figure out what law I had broken. There I sat, in tears because of something tangible, and in fear of something I could not predict.

The officer waved as he passed by on his way to the real emergency and I slumped back in my seat, one prayer answered, now officially and completely done with this day. I checked for traffic, signaled, and found my way around the corner to my house. Part of me hoped that I'd see her car in the driveway, but I didn't. Part of me hoped that I'd missed a call or a text from her, but I hadn't. I pulled into the driveway and went inside, using her key to enter the house.

I dropped my bag on the couch, poured myself a glass of water, and walked upstairs to my bedroom where I changed into some basketball shorts and an old t-shirt. The ones she used for pajamas were still folded up on her pillow. The lounge clothes she wore around the house were still hanging up in her portion of the closet, which reminded me that I still had some clothes at her place as well. I secretly hoped that she wouldn't ask me to come get them, because that might mean I still had a chance to apologize and tell her the truth, no matter how foolish it sounded.

I could smell her as I lay down on the bed. I closed my eyes and the first memory I had of her was there. I could see it as though I were one of the other patrons in the coffee shop that day. I looked at her and knew as soon as I caught her that she was the person I was going to marry. The second I touched her arm, I could feel the warmth of her love and I knew I was hers if she'd have me. She and I were destined to meet that day. I just never thought that this would be part of our story. I thought about the first few dates. I thought about taking her home to meet Mom and Dad. I thought about New Year's Eve, and the conversation I'd had with her dad. He told me that trust was everything, and I had not only failed her, I had failed him too. I'd told her sister that I would always take care of her and I hadn't done that. She said she needed space, but I needed to apologize. I didn't think it would make her change her mind, that wasn't my intention at all. I just knew that my actions yesterday were not a reflection of how I felt and I needed her to know that I knew I was wrong.

I picked up the phone and opened the messages app. I scrolled back through our messages and laughed at our inside jokes. She was the one person I wanted to talk to about what I was feeling, and yet the one person I couldn't speak with at all. *How on earth did I let this happen?* I started typing a message to her and deleted it. I started over again and stopped. I rephrased my words about 20 times, none of them feeling adequate enough to express what I was feeling. None of them feeling appropriate enough for the moment. None of them gave her the one thing that she asked for, which was space. So I deleted every single word, closed the app, and set my phone on top of her pillow. One deep sigh and I was off to sleep, which is probably what I needed to do in the first place. I hoped that my dreams wouldn't haunt me, but I felt like I deserved it if they did.

———

Dr. Chris:

The first night was the worst night. He dropped me off at the condo after the argument and I was afraid to get out of the truck. So we sat in the circle drive for a minute or two which caught Ralph's attention. He came to the door of the truck and offered to help me out and I politely declined.

"I have to go, Charlie, or he's going to come back and ask you to move Chief. You can't park here for more than a minute."

He nodded and hopped out of the truck to open the door for me. Once he was in front of the truck, I opened the door myself. He offered his hand to help me out and I accepted it, one last time. He reeled me in for a hug like he always did, but this one felt different. We held onto each other in the chilly April air, hugging like this would be the last time we'd ever see each other. He held me like he wasn't coming back and I sobbed into his shoulder at the thought that this would be it.

He had no words. There was nothing coming out of his mouth. He only held me like this was it. There we stood on Easter Sunday, each waiting for the other to let go. Each wanting to hold on forever. I didn't want this to be it. I didn't want this to be the end of us, but I didn't want to beg him to see me.

"Charlie," I said into the air. He loosened his grip and gingerly held my face in his hands, kissing me like tomorrow wasn't promised and he needed me to know that he loved me today. And I felt it. But he wasn't telling me what he was feeling. Saying it was equally as important as demonstrating those words.

Time and patience had proven themselves to be the ultimate storyteller. By the time we got to the end of the our story, time and patience had given up. We were marching towards a goal that was no longer in sight, which meant we were simply roaming along. Tears had found their way down my cheeks again as he kissed me and I held on to the outside of his hands, which still cupped my face. I broke from his embrace and looked him in the eyes, so much pain in there.

"Are we really doing this?" he asked softly, his voice cracking as he spoke.

I tried to be strong. "Charlie, I have to go."

"Chris?" His words were still soft but definitely a bit stronger in force, "are we really doing this?" he asked again.

"I can't pretend like I don't want more," I told him. "The more I wanted it, the further away from it we got."

"Chris," he said tenderly.

I let go of his hands. "I can't do this, Charlie."

He dropped his hands from my face and placed them in his pockets. "You're breaking my heart, Chris. You know I want more. I've told you that since Day 4. DAY FOUR!!"

"Then why are we still here?" I paused awaiting an answer that I knew wouldn't come. "I'm walking in place and you're walking backwards."

"Chris."

"I can't do this."

"Chris."

"I need some time, Charlie."

"Chris."

"Just give me some time, Charlie."

He pulled the key from his pocket and tried to give it back, but I wouldn't accept it. I wouldn't even look at it. Instead I rolled his fingers up around it, tucking it inside his fist like a ball. He watched me walk away. I know because I peered back at him for just a moment, to remember him leaning against his blue pickup truck, waiting for me to turn around and change my mind. I loved him deeply, but I loved myself enough to hold the line.

I thanked Ralph for keeping an eye out and headed up to R227. I sat on the end of my bed and glanced at his pajamas, still resting on the corner of his side of the bed. I wondered if he understood what I needed. I wondered if he understood my point. I wondered if he was done-done, or if he still wanted me. I wondered if any of it mattered. I sighed deeply and fell on the bed where I drifted off to sleep for a few hours, waking only to the sound of my phone which turned out to be my sister, asking why we had stood up the entire family at Easter dinner. I had to explain the entire situation to her which further exhausted me and I went to sleep again after getting off the phone with her.

"Tell Mom for me?"

"I will sis. Be patient with him."

"I'm trying," I said through more tears.

The next day I picked up my phone to text him and let him know that I was thinking about him when I saw the bouncing text bubbles that let me know he was typing a message, so I waited. They'd start then stop. Start again, then disappear. Start, stop, start, stop. Either he had a really long message or he was editing it along the way. I watched it for a good 10 minutes but eventually they disappeared all together, which meant he had changed his mind. That was definitely not a good day.

That night I thought about the words his mother had whispered in my ears as we prepared to head back to Kansas City on the morning after Christmas. He had asked me what she said and I promised her that I'd never tell him. But I understood her message in this moment. It made sense before, but I was full of clarity after having some time away to think.

"You have to tell him what you want. Be as clear as a bell. He'll listen because he loves you that much."

Every day that followed was equally as hard and then I turned a corner. I stopped focusing so much on what I missed about him and turned my attention to a celebration of what we had shared together. It was pretty miraculous that such a chain of events could string themselves together and give the two of us the opportunity to meet by chance. It was even more miraculous that our lives were already intertwined and designed to meet again because of a child who linked the two of us together. He was still home, even though it had been a couple of weeks since I'd seen him.

As full Spring made itself known, the world gave us fresh grass and new leaves, and rose buds, and other floral blossoms. It was a great reminder of the changes that were necessary for life to continue. Old things were made new again through a shedding of sorts. There was discomfort before things were made whole and I wondered if that applied to relationships as well.

———

Charlie:

I sat in the bed of my truck at her favorite spot on the lake, reflecting on all that was new in the world. Things hadn't gotten any easier in the past couple of weeks, but they had become more clear. I didn't know how much time I was supposed to give her, or if I was supposed to say something or if she was going to speak up when she was ready. I didn't know any of that. I only knew that she was still my heart and I had to fight to get her back.

I kept thinking about the moment I dropped her off at the condo. We sat in the truck not wanting to move, then Ralph came and busted up the mood, just as I was about to blurt out how I felt. So she moved things outside. I held on for as long as I could. I showed her that I loved her through my kiss. I gave her my heart in action, but she wouldn't let me say the words.

I asked if we were really doing this and she told me that she had to go. I asked her again, "Chris, are we really doing this?" and she told me that she couldn't pretend like she didn't want more, that the more she wanted it, the further away from us it got. I called her name so I could tell her how I felt.

She let go of my hands, so I took my hands off of her face and reached into my pocket to remove the ring from the box. I told her that she was breaking my heart, because she was. She knew how I felt about her. I'd told her that since the beginning of time. She said I was walking backwards. Backwards, I questioned with what I knew to be in my pocket.

I held the ring in my hand within my pocket and called her name again, trying for just a second to get her to listen to me so I could tell her what she meant to me and what I wanted for us. She told me she couldn't do it. I tried again to get her to listen. She told me she needed time. I called her name again, desperate to get her to hear me. She asked for some time. It was clear that she wasn't going to hear me out, so I pulled the ring from my pocket and tried to hand it to her. She didn't even look at it, she just rolled it up in my hand like it was nothing and walked away. I had been carrying this ring with me since March. It felt like it was burning a hole in my pocket. I had been waiting for the right time. But in that moment I knew it was highly likely that there might never be another opportunity and she wouldn't even acknowledge what I had attempted to give her.

The entire scene played out in my mind over and over again like reel-to-reel footage. I watched her walk away like she was going to realize there was a ring in my hand and turn around to come jump in my arms. That didn't happen. She walked away. I watched her talk to Ralph. I watched her get on the elevator. I watched the doors of the elevator close and dropped my head. I slipped the ring back in the box before getting back in the truck and driving away from my heart. I drove to my house, which was no longer home.

In the days and weeks that followed, I still kept the box on me at all times, hoping that I'd run into her again and that I could properly spill my guts from one knee, not during an argument. I needed her to understand that I had every intention of always taking care of her. This time away from each other made it crystal clear what my priorities were and what they should have been. I knew if I ever had the chance to see her again, that's what I'd tell her. I tried visiting the Fresh Grind to see if I could catch her trying to buy another cider with sugarplums, but it was Spring, and they didn't sell cider during the springtime. I'd hoped to catch her during lunch at the Fresh Pantry, but that never quite panned out as planned either. Through all the failed sitings I remained hopeful. I'm not sure how to explain it, but hope was the only thing that kept me going.

As time passed, I received phone calls from her dad, checking to see how I was doing and if I'd seen her yet. I received calls from my mom, who was checking on me to see if I had contacted her yet and encouraging me not to let too much time pass. I received calls from Marlo, and Steve, checking in to see how I was doing. I received calls from Sabrina and Jax, just "calling to say hello" and check on me with their nosy behinds so they could report it to Steve who didn't want to call me twice in one week. I loved them all for loving both of us. They kept me centered and gave me a mission. It was a mission I was completely uncertain about the logistics of, but it was a mission nonetheless.

It turns out I needed this time to grow into who and what I wanted to be, so I could figure out what type of person I wanted to be in a relationship, and so I could become that person for Dr. Chris, if she'd still have me.

CHAPTER 15

MOTHER'S DAY

Dr. Chris:

It had been about a month since Easter. I was supposed to see my parents that evening. Well, we were supposed to see them that evening, but everything went downhill faster than a skier attempting to break an Olympic record. I was so glad to spend some time with them today. A lot had happened since I last saw them. I was a stronger person than I was before. Don't get me wrong, I'm not saying I was weak when I was with Charlie. However, I am stronger now for sticking to my guns.

I assumed this Mother's Day that we'd be spending time at Mom and Dad's house like normal, but Mom didn't want the mess associated with family that comes over and doesn't clean up behind themselves - like we sometimes did. So she had arranged for all of us, Vonne, the twins, and Jason included since he was home on leave, to have a Mother's Day brunch at a local black-owned restaurant. Since there were so many of us, Mom decided that she was going to reserve a room to ensure we didn't have to wait for an hour for tables to become available. That was the plan she had sent me via text when I asked her what she wanted to do on Mother's Day.

I woke up that morning feeling refreshed after finally sleeping more than 2 hours straight. Every night before that had been much of the same. Sleep, dream, wake, lie restless, repeat. Last night though, I had the same dream I awoke from the night before my birthday except this one was even more vivid than the first time.

In this dream, I was with my family and out of the blue Charlie was standing beside me. I could feel him before I saw him. His presence was strong and comforting. It was love and it was home. I felt engulfed by the sense of his very being and turned my head just enough to check my periphery. He reached for my hand and held it gently without saying a word. I didn't turn towards him. I didn't get a complete look at him, and still I knew it was him. I allowed him to hold my hand as the two of us stood with my family. Not a single word spoken between us but I felt his thoughts traveling from his hand through mine. When I turned my head to look him in the eyes he had dropped to one knee. In my dream, the location and the people faded into indiscernible expressionist paintings. It was just the two of us in that moment. His message continued to be sent through his hand and because it was a dream, of course I understood all of it. Not only that, I also had the supernatural ability to communicate back in the same way - through my fingers. So the two of us held an entire full-length conversation as I stood and he kneeled, using only the messages we were haptically communicating to each other. In both versions of the dream, this one and the original, I awoke just after Charlie had asked me to hold his heart until it grows old.

As I sat up in bed, I grabbed my phone to send three text messages. The first, to my mom, "Happy Mother's Day, Mom!! Thank you for nurturing my dreams." The second, to my sister, "Happy Mother's Day, sis! You are doing a phenomenal job raising the twins. I can hardly wait to see the amazing humans they grow to become thanks to all the love you pour into them."

The third, was to my other Mom, whom I had secretly been communicating with since meeting her, and even more so after telling Charlie that I needed some time. She was one of the first people I contacted afterwards. I thanked her for welcoming me into their family and expressing my regret over losing the opportunity to spend more time with them. She encouraged me to hold the line during those times I expressed doubt that I had made the right decision to request some space. She sent inspirational messages when I was on her mind and I sent recipes and the latest unconventional workouts I was doing at the moment.

She had become a bonus mother for me and still called me daughter even after her son and I weren't on speaking terms. So I sent her a message, "Mom, wishing you a very Happy Mother's Day! Thanks for everything!" and I got out of bed.

That morning I worked out in front of my tv, got some breakfast in my system, then got cleaned up and prepared to meet my family for brunch. The restaurant wasn't far from downtown, but I still made sure to leave so I had enough time to arrive, find a parking spot, and find my family on time, which meant early.

When I arrived, I told the hostess which party I was meeting and she smiled and guided me to the back room. I greeted my family with lots of love and hugs, and noticed that the table was set for far more than the seven of us that they told me were coming.

There was a wall of windows facing the street and an adjoining wall filled with artwork. Below the artwork was a string of tables filled with plates that led to the hot foods like pancakes and French toast, which beget the breakfast meats and eggs, then flowed into plates full of fresh fruit and bowls of salad. Beside that was a plate of pastries, then butter, flatware and napkins, which spilled into the beverage section. Glasses for water or juice were followed by mugs and what looked to be a fountain of steaming cider, complete with a bowlful of sugarplums sitting beside it glistening in the light of the sun. I looked back at the seating arrangement.

There were 5 additional empty seats

around the table. I looked to Dad who pursed his lips and pointed to Mom while chuckling. I glanced at Mom, who was trying to get me to sit down in a very specific chair. I was still standing in spite of her insistence.

"Who else is coming to brunch today?" I asked before I heard the voices of Grandma Elizabeth and Grandpa Charles behind me.

They were thanking the hostess for seating them. Behind them quickly trailed Charlie's parents, all of whom greeted me with a hug and a kiss to my cheek before greeting everyone else in the room and having a seat at the table. I looked to my sister Vonne for answers. She pretended to be preoccupied with Corwin and Christina, and poor Jason asked me directly not to look at him because he had just gotten home two nights prior.

I didn't know what was going on, but I could count. There was one more open chair immediately beside the one my mom had attempted to get me to sit in before Charlie's family arrived. I looked around the restaurant but didn't see him anywhere. I grabbed the back of my chair, but before

I could sit down I felt it. It was just like the dream.

———

Charlie:

I'd had regular conversations with my mom in the weeks leading up to Mother's Day. She always began each chat the same way, "How's Chris, Charlie?"

My response was always the same, "You tell me, Mom. I know you're still talking to her."

She'd laugh and tell me, "Maybe I am, maybe I'm not."

Though Mom refused to give me updates after their conversations, I knew that she was still connected. It was encouraging to me to know that. I knew that I wanted to follow up with her and I knew I needed help to do so. So I elicited the assistance of our families to get her in the room with me. They took it to an entirely different level. Mom told me the location and the time, and I was confused as to why they had opted for Mother's Day to foster our reconnection. I would eventually be far more confused than that, but I'll get to that momentarily.

I woke up that morning after struggling to sleep. I was anxious and nervous, and excited, and hopeful, and slightly fearful, but more than anything else I was grateful. I was grateful to have family and extended family who were willing to help. I was grateful for the opportunity to feel. I was grateful for the space and the opportunity to grow. I was grateful for the opportunity to share my thoughts with her, and even though nothing had transpired yet, I was grateful for whatever the outcome may be, whether it aligned with my hopes or not.

I sent my mom and grandmother text messages wishing them a Happy Mother's Day and letting them know that I'd call them later that afternoon. Then I carried on with my new morning routine.

I had turned to yoga to help with centering my thoughts and my body to start the day and it had helped me feel grounded. So I started this Mother's Day with the practice of yoga and concluded that practice with respect and reverence and the centering thought, Namasté. I had practiced creating space to respect the light and love within others, to recognize their soul and honor the space within them where the universe dwells. When my ego was charting the course, I didn't have the patience to do any of those things, which had ultimately led me to the head space I was currently in.

So I got cleaned up and hustled to get to the assigned location at the assigned time. The closer I got, the more I battled with my nerves. But the louder my nerves became, the more I centered myself in the thought that I was only going to share with her that my soul recognized her soul, and apologize for breezing past its existence before, which helped to quell their bubbly energy.

When I arrived at the location I saw her car immediately amongst all the others. I also thought I saw my father's truck, but shrugged it off as a coincidence. He and I had the same truck in a different color, but so did hundreds of thousands of others in the Midwest and the south. I straightened my tie, fixed the bouquet of honeysuckle stems, purple hydrangea heads and light red carnations, and walked into the space where I knew Dr. Chris would be waiting for me.

When I arrived at the front, the hostess asked me for the party I was joining and I used Dr. Chris' last name. A broad smile panned across her face as she asked me to follow her back to a private room. I could see her there, standing behind a chair, the room filled with our families; her sister and the twins, her parents, my parents, my grandparents. I loved them, all of them, but in that moment there was only one person I wanted to see.

I couldn't see her face, but I could see her light. As I stopped behind the chair beside her, I could feel the warmth of her soul. It was the same warmth that was present when I caught her that night. It was the same warmth that existed when I was at Jax's follow up appointment. It was the same warmth that I had felt when she snuggled behind me at the streetcar stop. It was the same warmth that had made itself known on Christmas Day, and Valentine's Day, and her birthday, and everyday between them. It was the same warmth that I had felt until the moment the elevator doors closed on Easter. It was ever present and I was grateful to have the chance to feel it one more time. She stood upright, like her senses had been triggered and her head turned ever so slightly in my direction. It felt like she was checking her blind spot.

I reached out for her hand and the energy was almost stronger than I was prepared for. I practiced breathing like I had done in my daily yoga sessions, to keep me calm and centered and focused on the goal; honoring her soul. She was gracious and welcomed my hand in hers and in that moment I felt love return to my heart.

———

Dr. Chris:
I felt his hand touch mine and the feeling of home was back instantaneously. He and I had much to discuss, but he approached me gently, as if to let me know that first and foremost, he saw me. I didn't want to look at him yet. I wanted first to soak in the moment. Our families sat around the table together pretending like they didn't see us holding hands and ignoring us so we could focus solely on each other.

He didn't open his mouth but I felt his apology come through his hand. I didn't say a word to him, but I thanked him for his apology. He intertwined his fingers between mine and just like the dream, the two of us held a complete conversation with each other without saying a word and without me ever looking at him.

What I heard and what I said follows.

He cupped my hand, "I'm sorry, Chris."

I closed the gap between our palms, "I know, Charlie."

He ran his thumb over my fingers, "I didn't honor you or your experience in our relationship."

I tapped his hand lightly with my thumb, "I appreciate the feedback and…"

He clasped his fingers between mine, "Please look at me, Chris."

"I'm too fearful to do that, Charlie," I said while flexing my fingers between his.

"I'm holding your hand through it. I'll be right here when you turn around. All of me will be here when you turn around," he said rubbing my thumb with his again.

"Promise?" I asked with a squeeze.

"Always," he promised with a reassuring squeeze and slight sway.

I finally turned around to look at him. His eyes were honest, and his face more handsome than I remembered. He looked different, stronger internally, but he was still home.

———

Charlie:

She and I held hands and looked around the room at our families as they attempted to give us space in a place where there was none to be had. I hadn't planned all of this, but I appreciate whomever was thoughtful enough to think through these details. I had made myself a promise that I would apologize and if her soul felt receptive to it that I would tell her how I felt. I hoped that I could communicate with her without everyone else hearing what I had to say. It was supposed to be a private conversation, but I worked with what we were given. I sent my thoughts spiraling down to her hand in hopes that she would be able to understand.

I apologized to her first. After a moment,

she acknowledged my apology and I sent another message. I told her the truth about where I had failed myself, and in doing so where I had failed us. She thanked me for sharing, and I asked her to turn around and look at me. She expressed her fear of doing so. I promised her that I was with her, that she wasn't alone, that I would be fully present with her when she looked at me. She asked if I could promise her that and I told her that I would always be fully present.

She turned around and saw me, all of me. Her face was receptive. Her soul was open. I knew this was it. My gut told me that I'd know it, and this was it. I placed the flowers on the floor as I dropped to one knee right there in front of our families, in front of the other restaurant patrons, and most importantly, in front of her.

———

Dr. Chris:

It was just like the dream. He dropped to one knee, never breaking eye contact with me. Everything around us looked like a painting you'd find hanging in a museum. He and I were alone amongst company. The difference between the dream and reality is that he spoke his thoughts aloud after dropping to his knee.

"Christina James, I've known from the moment you knocked me into all those other people that I wanted to be your partner spiritually and as we walk this earth. I have grown leaps and bounds in love and in being since you entered my life, and I'm grateful for all you've poured into me. I appreciate you holding my feet to the fire when I wasn't standing as your partner. I love you for loving me enough to ask me to be a better human. You helped me to become whole individually so I can be present with you and strong for us. You are love and you are my lighthouse.

The truth is, that evening when I caught you, you actually caught me. Our souls have been tied together since that moment and I would be honored to have the opportunity to encourage your wildest dreams and weather the storms of life together. I love you deeply, Chris, with everything that's in me. I promise you, as long as there is breath in my lungs that you'll never be alone if you're willing to walk with me. Hold my heart until it grows old?"

Charlie:

I reached into my pocket and pulled out the ring box that I'd been carrying with me since the night before her birthday. It held the same ring she had ignored before our break. The same ring that possessed so much more meaning for me in this moment than it ever had before. I presented the ring to her and she turned her head, responding with a smile, "Always."

"Will you allow me to marry you, Chris?"

Her hands cupped her face which had become flush with blood. Overcome with emotion, she started to fall and I quickly stood to catch her. I asked if she was okay.

"Yes, Charlie," she replied, her eyes full of love. I nodded, thankful that she hadn't fainted and hit the ground.

She repeated herself, "YES, Charlie."

I was so concerned about her condition

that I had forgotten I asked to marry her. "Yes?" I asked, wondering aloud what she was saying yes to.

"YES!" she replied with heavy emphasis that smacked me across the face and helped me remember the question I asked before she started to faint.

"YES?" I asked again, this time, for very specific clarification.

"Yes, sweetheart," she said, exuding the love and light that lived within her soul.

I covered my heart with my hand before placing the ring on her finger and kissing her like tomorrow wasn't promised and I needed her to know I loved her today.

———

Dr. Chris:
The rest of the world didn't come back into focus until after we finished kissing each other and I told Charlie I needed the stethoscope. It wasn't until then that I heard the applause of the other people in the restaurant, including my niece and nephew.

I saw the love that was evident in the faces of our parents and his grandparents, and we stood there holding each other for a while, afraid to move. Part of me was nervous that this was another dream that I'd awaken from momentarily, then I heard him whisper something in my ear that he never said in the other two dreams.

"Can I get your chair?"

I nodded as I sat down across from our parents who were filled with excitement as Charlie transferred the bouquet of flowers from the floor to my hand.

He apologized for not greeting everyone when he entered, then circled the room with hugs and wishes for a Happy Mother's Day.

I assumed he had pulled this entire thing together, but his questions let me know that he had been tricked just as much if not more than I was. We both had questions that we'd ask after everyone was able to fix a plate at the buffet and after Grandpa Charles said a special prayer.

"Dear Lord, we thank you for bringing us all back together on this very special

Mother's Day. We thank You for healed hearts, safe returns, and new beginnings. May we always remember Your love in everything we do. We thank You for the food we are about to receive for the nourishment of our bodies. For Christ our Redeemer's sake, Amen!"

And the table concurred, "Amen!"

Charlie rose to fix me a mug of hot cider with a spoonful of sugarplums and I was enamored with the way the light continued to bounce and dance off of their exterior. Grandma Elizabeth watched the way I looked at the sugarplums and smiled in my direction, asking me if I remembered her question about whether or not I made the sugarplums that I had gifted them at Christmas.

"I do," I told her.

"Chris, my mother always told me where sugarplums shimmer, there is love. So, when you told me that you had prepared them yourself, I knew the two of you would be just fine."

"I forgot about that. Grandma used to

say that all the time," his dad remembered fondly. He turned towards the bowl of sugarplums, as did the rest of us, and we all admired the love that filled the room as the sugarplums continued to twinkle in the light of the sun.

———

Charlie:

I sat back in my chair after bringing Dr. Chris her mug of cider, re-centering the locket she had received from my mom before noticing that Mom was wearing hers on that day too. I took it all in. My parents were chatting with her parents. My grandparents were chatting across the table to Chris' twin niece and nephew. Her sister Vonne and her husband were gazing into each other's eyes after being separated by military orders for so long. I looked at Chris' face as she too was absorbing the moment. Soft music played in the background as did the sounds of those who were there to celebrate their moms with a special breakfast or lunch. Love really did grow here.

My plate was full of food, but I wasn't very hungry. I think I had been satiated by my surroundings. My arm wrapped around her, I rubbed Dr. Chris lightly on her shoulder as I gazed at the way her engagement ring caught the sun, reflecting and refracting its beams several times over. In that moment I drew a parallel between her glistening ring and the glint of the sugarplums in the corner. My heart was so full as I thought about all the times that sugarplums were reflective of love in our relationship and I couldn't help but smile at Grandma's recollection. It felt like divine intervention had led our families right here, to this moment, and I was grateful for it all. I was lucky enough to get to love Chris forever. Especially so because second chances don't always find their way around.

She and I would always have this day. We'd always have the love and support of our families, and we'd always have the wisdom of my great grandmother who was right, where sugarplums shimmer, there is love.

Author's Notes & Acknowledgments

Author's Notes

Tremendous thanks to all who encouraged me to write the second book in the Sugarplum series. I knew there was a second book to be written as soon as the first was finished, but I wasn't entirely sure where Dr. Chris and Charlie were headed, especially in the middle of a pandemic. I made a conscious decision to write from the perspective of the version of 2020 that most of us anticipated at the turn of the New Year. Maybe the challenges associated with navigating our new reality will be written into Book 3, but for this book it felt necessary to acknowledge and celebrate, all of the things we once took for granted.

———

Acknowledgments

To the Beta Readers; LaNee Bridewell, Tanesha Ford, Sophia Garcia, Denise Textor, and Manuela Villegas, and Kelly Williams, your feedback was invaluable. Thank you for donating your time and thoughts, to ensure that this book was dressed its best for its release date.

To my family and friends, thank you for encouraging my biggest dreams, especially in moments when I question their impact and validity. Your nudges are always right on time and I appreciate you more than you know. To Coach D, thanks for your steady and pushy support, and for encouraging me to crack open and share my heart with the world. To Herston, thank you for sharing your life with me for thirteen years.

Finally, to the enthusiastic readers of A Spoonful of Sugarplums, thank you for sharing your love of Dr. Chris and Charlie with me. I hope the sequel fills your heart with hope.

About the Author

C. L. Fails is an Author, Speaker, Creative Architect, and an Accidental Educator; having served pre-school through college students in her hometown of Kansas City. An agent for equity, she has dedicated her career to helping others learn to follow their internal compass, and thrive despite challenge. C. L. is currently Founder & CEO of LaunchCrate Publishing - a company created to help writers launch their work into the world while retaining the portion of profit they deserve. Outside of LaunchCrate she is an active advocate for education, serving as a former Girls on the Run Coach, on the Board of Directors for Junior Achievement of Greater Kansas City, as well as Chair Emeritus of the Multicultural Alumni Council at Kansas State University.

She is author and illustrator of the Ella Book Series, The Christmas Cookie books, and her latest series, "The Secret World of Raine the Brain." She also penned the interactive Modern Memoir, "So, Okay..." documenting the life stories of her then 94 year old Grandfather. All are fun books that inspire us to be bold, take risks, and learn from our mistakes. When she's not helping clients, hosting a podcast, speaking with audiences or working on her latest book about building community, you can find her doodling on whatever object may be nearby.

www.ingramcontent.com/pod-product-compliance
Lightning Source LLC
Chambersburg PA
CBHW010347170726
48284CB00011B/2812